The Hockey Farmer

by
Farhan Devji

Cacoethes Books are published by

Cacoethes Publishing House, LLC.
14715 Pacific Avenue South
Suite 604
Tacoma, WA 98444

Copyright © 2008 by Cacoethes Publishing House, LLC.
Copyright © 2008 by Farhan Devji

All rights reserved. No part of this book may be reproduced in any form or by any means without the prior written consent of the Publisher, excepting brief quotes used in reviews.

All Cacoethes titles imprints and distributed lines are available at special quantity discounts for bulk purchases for sales promotion, premiums, fund-raising, educational or institutional use.

Special book excerpts or customized printings can also be created to fit specific needs. For details, write or phone the office of the Cacoethes Sales Manager:
Cacoethes Publishing House, LLC.
14715 Pacific Avenue South, Suite 604
Tacoma, WA 98444.
Attn. Sales Department.
Phone: 253-536-3747
ISBN: 978-0-9818298-6-6

Printed in the United States of America

This book is a work of fiction. The names, characters, places and incidents are products of the writer's imagination or have been used fictitiously and are not to be construed as real. Any resemblance to persons, living or dead, actual events, locale or organizations is entirely coincidental.

Warning: This book may contain mild language.

Cacoethes Publishing House, LLC.
14715 Pacific Avenue South
Suite 604
Tacoma, WA 98444

The Hockey Farmer
Copyright © 2008 by Farhan Devji
Cover by Mia Romano
ISBN: 978-0-9818298-6-6
www.cacoëthespublishing.com

All Rights Are Reserved. No part of this book may be used or reproduced in any manner whatsoever without written permission, except in the case of brief quotations embodied in critical articles and reviews.

*A life on the farm and a life on the ice;
so different, yet so alike…*

The Hockey Farmer
By Farhan Devji

Growing up in Cochrane, Alberta—a large town located 22 km west of Calgary—Logan Watt's life consisted of essentially two things: Farming and Hockey. Naturally there was room for girls somewhere in his busy schedule too. And Logan wouldn't have it any other way. After getting passed up on by all 30 teams in the National Hockey League Entry Draft and breaking up with his first only girlfriend, Logan took on a new project for the upcoming summer, the rehabilitation of the legendary family farm. Little did he know that this one summer would have major implications on the rest of his professional and social life.

Dedicated to:

"The Hockey Farmer" is dedicated to all those who have (or at one point have had a dream to) become a professional sports athlete.

Acknowledgements

First and foremost, Farhan would like to thank his family, Bob, Azee and Shaheed for their support and encouragement in his aspirations to become a writer. Farhan would also like to thank Charles Baker because if it wasn't for him, Farhan would have never even considered writing a novel. Lastly, Farhan would like to thank everyone who throughout his eighteen years of existence has had any sort of positive or negative effect on him in any way, shape, or form.

Chapter 1

"With the first overall selection in the 2008 National Hockey League Entry Draft, the New York Islanders are pleased to select, from the Russian Super League, Demitri Shirokov."

Watching the Entry Draft on his 25-inch television at his home in Cochrane, Alberta, Logan Watt imagined what it would be like to hear his name called by a representative of any National Hockey League team. Logan didn't bother making the trip down to Ottawa to attend the draft, even though he had a slight chance of being chosen in one of the later rounds. It wasn't that the draft wasn't important to him, but he just didn't see the point in getting all worked up over something he couldn't control.

The average Canadian kid dreams of hearing his name called by a General Manager at the National Hockey League Entry Draft, and Logan Watt was no exception. Growing up in Cochrane, Alberta—a large town located 22 kilometres west of Calgary—Logan played amateur hockey with the Midget AAA Flames. This past season, Logan was his team's captain; he led the entire league in goals and assists, and he was also named the Most Valuable Player of the league. But Logan's problem was that players in Cochrane, Alberta didn't get as much recognition or attention from the professional scouts as players from the

The Hockey Farmer

Canadian Hockey League did. The Canadian Hockey League was for all the elite players between the age of 17 to 20 and was a big step from playing amateur hockey in Cochrane. For that reason, Logan had his doubts that he would be drafted. And his small stature of 5'9" wouldn't help his cause either.

"I'm going to go feed the chickens," said Jacob, Logan's father. "You should come with me; you can't sit glued to the couch watching TV all day, especially when it's so nice out."

That was one thing Logan already knew. He was a big fan of the outdoors, and sitting inside while the sun shone brightly outside was killing him. He wasn't planning on watching the whole draft anyway, but today he wasn't in the farming mood either.

"I just want to see when Mark gets drafted, and then I think I'm going to hit up the Big Hill," said Logan.

Mark Simpson was one of Logan's best friends from childhood; they'd played together for six years in the Cochrane minor hockey system before Mark was offered a contract with the Calgary Hitmen of the Western Hockey League. Mark had impressed many professional scouts during his last two seasons with the Hitmen and was expected to be a top ten pick in this year's NHL Entry Draft. A considerable part of his appeal was his tremendous core strength; he and Logan were both fitness junkies, so to speak. They were always in the best of shape, due largely in part to their respective training regimes. They used to cycle up to the Big Hill together, which was a very popular training ground for cyclists from the Cochrane region.

"With the tenth selection in the 2008 National Hockey League Entry Draft, the Toronto Maple Leafs are pleased to select, from the Calgary Hitmen of the Western Hockey League, Mark Simpson."

Logan was thrilled when he heard Mark's name called—he knew how hard Mark had worked to get where he was, and he felt as though he himself had also accomplished something. But dragging along with that sense of accomplishment was a hint of jealousy, which was only natural. Logan and Mark had gone through all the same steps together when it came to hockey, and Logan couldn't help but be envious of what Mark was on the verge of accomplishing. However, he wasn't resentful or bitter—that just wasn't in his nature. If anything, Mark's success gave Logan something to strive for; it gave him a sense of optimism and hope.

The NHL Entry Draft was seven rounds long with a two-minute break squeezed between each of the thirty teams' picks, and after ten picks of the first round, Logan had already seen enough. He'd wanted to see Mark get drafted, and that's what he'd done; he knew that if he himself were to get drafted, it certainly wouldn't be for another couple of hours. Logan also knew he would rather go on another one of his cycling expeditions than be a couch potato for the whole day.

"Alright, Dad, I'm off to the Big Hill. Should be back in an hour or two," Logan yelled as he walked along the dirt path on his way to the storage barn.

It actually wasn't much of a barn; it was more of a storage garage where Logan kept his bike and all of his hockey equipment. When he was younger, while Jacob worked on the farm, Logan used to have all his friends over to play hockey in the barn. This was convenient for Jacob too, because he spent most of the day in or around the

The Hockey Farmer

grading station directly adjacent from the barn, so he was able to keep a close watch on the kids from there. Some nights, Logan would stay in the barn for hours practicing his shot all alone before his father had to drag him inside. Whenever Logan wasn't in the barn playing hockey, he was playing hockey with his amateur hockey team or helping his father on the farm. Logan's two biggest passions were hockey and farming. Some days he played hockey for hours, some days he worked on the farm for hours, and some days he just did a combination of the two. But he would rarely be found doing anything that wasn't involved with hockey or farming in one way or another.

As he cycled up the Big Hill, Logan wondered what types of emotions were going through Mark's mind. But his train of thought was ended abruptly when Logan received more than a few awkward stares when his Backstreet Boys ring-tone went off at the exact moment he reached the top of the hill. A sudden shiver ran down his spine.

This could be the call, Logan thought as he checked his watch, quickly trying to figure out what round the draft would be in at this time.

"Now this is why I need call display," he said aloud as he received a few more awkward looks from the teenage girls walking by.

He took an extended deep breath and answered the phone.

"Hello," he said.

"Logan, I need some help moving these crates; do you think you could give me a hand when you're done?"

It was Jacob. Typically, Logan was the type of kid who didn't mind receiving a call from his father, but under these circumstances, he was understandably disappointed.

"Sure, I'll be back down in a bit," said Logan, with an apparent tone of discontent in his voice.

When Logan returned to the farm, he decided he would promptly get an update about the draft situation before helping his father transfer the crates. He signed in on the computer and immediately noticed an abundance of unread e-mails—which surprised him, since Logan usually stayed on top of his e-mail. Logan opened up his mailbox, hoping to find some messages congratulating him on being drafted, but he instead found twenty-five new group invitations from Facebook. Apparently the local radio station in Cochrane was running a contest that rewarded whoever could get the most members in their group with a $1500 bursary, and apparently several of Logan's friends had taken interest in the contest. Since Facebook was the last thing on Logan's mind at the moment, he quickly closed the window and proceeded to the National Hockey League's official website. He swiftly scanned through all the names, but didn't see his own. He examined the names a second time, a little more carefully, but was still unable to find his name. The draft was finished, and so were Logan's hopes and dreams of being drafted in the NHL. Logan's break-up with his girlfriend, now combined with the draft disappointment, started his summer off on not quite the right foot.

"You have to remember that many elite players in the NHL were never drafted, so this doesn't have to be the end of the line for you when it comes to hockey," said Jacob as he and Logan walked along a dirt path with several crates stacked in their hands.

The Hockey Farmer

"But on the other hand, you already know how much I would love for you to help me re-habilitate, and ultimately take over, the family farm," Jacob added.

Logan didn't respond. He was already thinking about what his father had said. Logan had always thought he was destined to play professional hockey, but now he started to question if what he'd originally considered his destiny was, in reality, merely a childhood dream. He began to ask himself whether he had the skill or size to make it to the next level. He started to wonder if he was actually destined to stay in Cochrane, Alberta for the rest of his life and take over the legendary family farm rather than leave home and become a professional hockey player.

Chapter 2

For about two and a half years, Jacob had been pleading with Logan to help him re-establish and rehabilitate their family farm. Jacob didn't really have the financial luxury to hire anyone to help them, so he'd been waiting for Logan to find the time. It wasn't that Logan didn't want to aid his father in the restoration of the family's pride; on the contrary, he would have loved to spend a summer doing just that but was never able to because of his heavy workload in school, coupled with his busy hockey schedule. Seeing as Logan had nothing special planned this summer, he realized that this could be the perfect opportunity for him to finally satisfy his father's wishes. Logan also thought spending a summer working on the farm, day in and day out, would help him determine whether he would be content doing this for the rest of his life or if he should continue to pursue his childhood dream of playing in the National Hockey League.

"Are you sure?" said Jacob when Logan told his father of his plans. "You're not going to pull out halfway through the summer, are you now?" he added, knowing full well that Logan was the type of kid who would always stay true to his word.

"By the end of this summer, the farm will be in stellar shape once again. I'm going to make sure of it,"

The Hockey Farmer

said Logan. He saw a big smile come across his father's face, reassuring Logan that he made the right decision.

"Does this mean you're going to give up you dream to play in the..." began Jacob, but Logan cut him off. Logan knew what his father was about to ask him, and quite frankly, he wasn't ready to answer that question yet. All Logan wanted to do was forget about all the important decisions he would have to make and just focus on the farm and see where that took him.

"This doesn't mean anything," responded Logan. "I'm going to help you on the farm this summer because that's what I want to do, but after that, your guess is as good as mine—I just don't know."

Jacob realized he was pushing all the wrong buttons with his son, and that was not his intention. While Jacob would love having Logan on the farm for the rest of his life, he knew that if Logan wasn't happy, he wouldn't be either. If Logan decided he wanted to make another attempt to put together a National Hockey League career, Jacob would fully support him. Aside from his two-and-a-half year ambition to rehabilitate the farm, all Jacob wanted was to see his only son succeed.

As Logan watched the Calgary Flames face off against the Edmonton Oilers in the notorious "Battle of Alberta," he wondered how it would feel to play hockey in front of thousands of die-hard fans either cheering you or jeering you. The most spectators at one of Logan's games had been about two hundred, and at the time Logan had thought that was something special. From the age of five, Logan, along with his father, had made it a tradition to sit down in their living room and watch Hockey Night in Canada every Saturday on their beloved 25-inch television.

Saturday was never a busy day on the farm for Jacob, and Logan had hockey practice bright and early in the morning, so it worked out perfectly for both of them. Oddly enough, Sunday was indeed a farming day for the Watt family.

"Tomorrow, we should probably get up around eight or nine o'clock," Jacob said as the Flames game came to an abrupt end in overtime. "We have a lot do, so it would probably be a good idea to get some rest."

"Yes, sir," answered Logan.

The next morning, Logan woke up at seven o'clock. He hadn't been able to sleep at all with the profusion of thoughts swirling around in his mind. All Logan wanted to do was focus on the farm, but he'd soon realized that it was easier said than done. Most teenagers in Logan's current situation, the dreadful summer following the Twelfth Grade, only worried about what party they were going to hit up the next night and which assortment of illegal substances they planned on abusing while there. Logan, on the other hand, was trying to decide what he wanted to do with his life. Logan wasn't socially inept—he was always one of the more popular and social kids in school, and he had several good friends—but he simply felt that this summer would be the building block for his future. That was what Logan had pondered the previous night while laying in his bed, wishing he was out for the count. And that's what he continued thinking about as he sat on the couch the next morning, waiting for Jacob's orders.

"The produce company should be arriving any minute now," Jacob told Logan. "I'll head off to the grading station to get all the machines set up, and then you can join me after you unload all the boxes."

"Yes, sir," Logan responded again.

The Hockey Farmer

Logan was a man of few words: He rarely spoke more than what was necessary, and that was a large reason why so many of his peers admired him. For that same reason, whenever Logan did have something to say, everyone listened.

The produce company would deliver a van full of boxes to the farm, jam-packed with several trays of eggs of many different sizes and varieties. Logan and Jacob's job was to make sure all the eggs were free of any spots or dirt; to separate the whites from the browns; to separate and organize the small, medium, and jumbo sized eggs; and to finally transfer them all to their respective cartons. From there, they would re-pack the cartons into the boxes, transport them into a van of their own, and deliver them all over town. It seemed like quite a simple process, and with the aid of all the upper echelon machinery in the grading station it was fairly straightforward—but that wasn't to say it was trouble-free and effortless. Grading the eggs would take a day and delivering them would usually take another unless they also had to deliver to Calgary, which would take another whole day in itself. The work ethic required to run a farm must be second to none, but luckily for Jacob and Logan, they were two good ole Canadian rednecks who knew how to put their work boots on, figuratively speaking.

"Good work today, son," said Jacob. "Tomorrow we'll hop in the van and deliver the eggs."

"I'll drive," replied Logan, exhausted.

"Ahh, we'll see about that," Jacob said before he headed back into the grading station to make sure all the machines were properly turned off.

That night, Logan wasn't able to sleep any better, even though he was completely drained physically and mentally. He wondered if he would be able to work on the farm like he had today for the rest of the summer, let alone for the rest of his life. He'd helped on the farm when he was younger, but never like this. Today, he'd gotten a real taste of what it was like to be a farmer, and he wasn't so sure he enjoyed it.

Chapter 3

Logan and Jacob went through the exact same process of grading and delivering eggs every single day—excluding Saturday, of course—for the next two weeks. And even though the days began to get longer and the workload continued to increase, Logan's inability to get a good night's sleep persisted. The produce company would bring in new stock every other day and expect it to be delivered to businesses all over town within 48 hours, which didn't leave a lot of downtime for Logan, let alone time for him to make a stop at the local rink or his "hockey barn" for some stick and puck action. On top of grading and delivering eggs, Logan and Jacob had to carry out several other tasks on the farm including mending fences, checking the waters, milking the cows, farming the tractors, feeding the chickens, collecting their eggs, maintaining the barns, and looking after all the paperwork. There was always something to do. Grading days would usually end at around four or five o'clock, and afterwards Logan and Jacob would attend to all of their other responsibilities. They generally did the grading together because it was almost impossible to do it alone, but they divided all the other tasks between the two of them. Jacob would milk the cows, feed the chickens, collect their eggs, and attend to the paperwork while Logan would carry out more of the extensive labour. He would farm the tractors, mend the fences, maintain the barns, and check the waters, all of which required a combination of strength, endurance, focus, and a tremendous work ethic.

Through the guidance of his father, coupled with his tireless efforts on the farm, Logan started to notice that without the right attitude or work ethic, he wouldn't be able to efficiently perform his tasks on the farm—or as a hockey player—for much longer. Fortunately for the well-being of the farm, this was something Jacob had been preaching to Logan for his entire life, and after working on the farm for the first few weeks of the summer, Logan began to understand this theory first-hand. He began to understand that a life on the farm and a life as a hockey player were of the same kind.

"Is there anything else that needs to be done?" asked Logan after he had completed all of his tasks for the day.

"You've done everything already?" replied Jacob as he checked his watch, wondering if he had lost track of the time. Much to his disbelief, he hadn't. It was only four-thirty, and Logan was suggesting he had nothing left to do. Jacob wondered if Logan had lost track of some his duties.

"Yes, sir," responded Logan, showing no sign of any emotion.

"Have you cleaned all the barns?" asked Jacob.

"Yes, sir," Logan responded once again, still inexpressive.

"Checked the waters?" asked Jacob.

"Yes, sir," responded Logan, this time with a tad bit of displeasure and irritation in his voice.

The Hockey Farmer

"Alright then. Well, the produce company just dropped off the stock for tomorrow, so I guess you could start carrying the boxes to the grading station, but…"

Logan promptly cut off his father. "I'll take care of it," he said as he grabbed another water bottle and started to walk toward the produce company's van.

As Jacob sat in his little office that was crammed between the kitchen and living room, he watched Logan walk towards the produce van through the window and wondered if Logan was still enjoying the farm work like he used to—because it sure didn't seem like it. It was hard not to notice that Logan had drastically upped his workload, but was he truly enjoying it? Jacob wondered if he had forced his son to do something he really didn't want to, which had not been part of the plan. After his wife died, when Logan was only five years old, his son was all that Jacob had left, along with his dearly loved farm. Jacob didn't want to see his son dejected; on the contrary, his only wish was to see his son happy. Was Logan only working on the farm to please his father, or was Jacob overthinking the situation? He decided to confront his son.

"Logan, can I speak to you for a minute?" asked Jacob.

"I'm almost done unloading the boxes—just give me a couple of minutes," replied Logan.

Jacob felt he had already waited long enough.

"Let me rephrase this, Logan: I need to speak to you for a minute," he said.

"What's up?" Logan asked as he put down the box. "Is there a problem with the paperwork?"

"The paperwork is fine," responded Jacob.

"Then what is it?" asked Logan, wondering what was so important that his father couldn't have waited a few more minutes.

"I've noticed you've really picked up your workload here on the farm," said Jacob.

Yeah, so what's the problem? Logan thought.

"And I've also noticed you don't seem to be enjoying it as much. Is there something you want to tell me?" asked Jacob.

"Nothing," replied Logan.

"You're not going to make this easy for me, are you now?" Jacob asked as Logan remained silent.

"Alright then, well, I'll get right to it," said Jacob. "If you don't want to work on the farm anymore, that's fine Logan. I understand. I know this is very hard work, and if you're not enjoying it as much as you did when you were younger, I won't hold it against you. If you want to start playing hockey again, I will support you one hundred percent."

After a long, awkward pause, Logan finally had something to say.

"I told you I would dedicate this summer to re-establishing the farm, and that's what I plan to do," he said, adding, "If I wasn't enjoying it, I wouldn't be doing it."

"So I'm completely overreacting and out of line to think you're not having fun?" asked Jacob.

"If I wasn't enjoying it, I wouldn't be doing it," Logan said a second time before he picked up the last of the boxes and carried them towards the grading station.

Jacob had never seen Logan act this way before. He seemed distant and uninterested in anything Jacob had to say. This summer, Logan seemed to be testier than a normal teenager, and Jacob didn't think his son's recent attitude change had anything to do with hormones—which only confirmed his fears that Logan was indeed not enjoying his summer.

As Logan lay in bed that night, he wondered if he had made a big mistake. His father had given him the perfect opportunity to back out, but he hadn't taken it. He didn't detest working on the farm, but admittedly, he was far from enjoying it. Logan didn't want to break the promise he'd made to his father at the beginning of the summer, so he would continue to work on the farm. But he also started to worry that this summer would ruin the passion he'd once had for farming. When Logan was younger, he'd helped his father in certain areas of the farm about once or twice a week, but he'd never had his own responsibilities resembling those he had this summer—hence why he wasn't enjoying it like he once did. Logan didn't want this one summer to take away from all his pleasant childhood memories, but he wasn't about to neglect the commitment he'd made either.

Well, I have nothing else important to do this summer anyways, and I've already done a great deal of work, so why stop now? Logan thought. *And no matter what my father says, I know nothing would make him happier than to finally have the farm up and running again.*

Much to his satisfaction, for the first time this summer, Logan slept like a baby. He had finally come to terms with the decision he had made. He would have undoubtedly loved to be in the same situation as his friend Mark, but he realized that a life on the farm, close to his family and friends, might not be so bad after all.

Chapter 4

Logan woke the next morning at eight o'clock on the dot. Feeling rejuvenated and rested from his good night's sleep, he made his way to the kitchen to grab a bagel or two before a new day's work on the farm. Logan wasn't much of a breakfast eater, which was pretty much the only weakness in his nutritional intake. Maybe this was genetic, because Jacob wasn't big on breakfast either. Logan wasn't a cereal fan and never had the time or energy to actually make something like toast or eggs, even with the surplus of eggs in the house. Ironically, Logan's work ethic was second to none when it came to farming and hockey, but when it came to the kitchen, he was as lazy as can be. A bagel or two with either strawberry or regular flavoured cream cheese would do the job for Logan, and he would make up for his diminutive breakfasts with oversized lunches and dinners. Back when Logan was a child, he'd always looked forward to his summer lunches, primarily because they got him out of the stuffy and malodorous grading station.

As Logan spread the cream cheese on both bagels, he heard his ring-tone go off in his bedroom, so he quickly put down the knife and made his way down the hall. Logan wondered who would be calling him so early in the morning on a summer weekday. None of his friends would

The Hockey Farmer

be awake at this time, and neither would any of his family from Calgary.

"Hello," Logan answered.

"Hey there, Logan; it's Hunter," said Logan's hockey coach from the past three seasons.

"Hey, Coach, how are you?" asked Logan.

"I'm great, and yourself?"

"Not too bad," said Logan. "What can I do for you?"

"Well, I have a proposition for you," Hunter said. "I don't know what your plans are for the upcoming season, but if you don't have anything planned yet, we would love to have you come back and help us coach the Midget AAA team."

"I'm honoured you came to me," Logan said, trying to stall as long as possible so he could think about the offer.

"You don't have to give me an answer right now," added Hunter. "As long as you let me know before the end of the summer, that's fine—but obviously, the sooner the better."

"I think this would be a great opportunity for me, but I have to figure out my plans before I make any concrete decisions. I wouldn't want to accept the offer now and then pull out halfway through the season, after I had already made a commitment to the team."

"That's completely understandable—just let me know when you've come to a decision," Hunter said.

"Sounds good," Logan replied.

"I look forward to hearing from you," Hunter said.

"Talk to you soon, Coach," Logan hung up the phone and made his way back to his unattended bagels.

As Logan polished off his two whole-grain bagels and made his way out the door en route to the unventilated grading station, he pondered the Coach's offer. He'd never pictured himself as coach material, but that didn't mean he wouldn't want to give it a try. The fact of the matter was, Logan was tempted to accept the offer for more than one reason: This job would allow him to stay close to home, to stay involved in the game he passionately loved, and at the same time to give back to the Cochrane minor hockey system which had done so much for him during his minor hockey years. Logan would love to share what he'd learned about the game of hockey with anyone who was willing to listen, and if Logan was the assistant coach, the players would listen. However, on the other side of the coin, if Logan accepted this job offer, he would basically say goodbye to his childhood aspirations to play in the National Hockey League. Because as an eighteen-year-old, if you miss a full season of playing hockey for any reason, the chances to take the next step are slim to none—and Logan was fully aware of this. It was pretty safe to say the good night's sleep Logan had received the previous night wouldn't become a regular habit.

While working diligently on the farm, Logan looked back on all of his memories playing minor hockey. Logan had started playing hockey at the Pee Wee level in Grade Seven, which was later than the majority of the kids. At that time, he didn't even play competitive hockey—he started off in the house league because he really had no idea how good he would be. That year, Logan wasn't the best player in the league, let alone the best player on his team; however, he improved a lot throughout the course of the regular season. Following that year, Logan played two

The Hockey Farmer

years at the Bantam level on the B team, which was a step up from the house league. Logan made huge strides during his two years on the B team, and that was when Hunter, the Midget AAA Coach, began to take notice of Logan's play. Near the end of Logan's final season at the Bantam level, Hunter approached him to make sure he would try out for the Midget AAA team the following season. Logan wasn't planning on trying out for the Triple A team, but when Hunter suggested that he should, Logan decided there was no harm in giving it a shot. Fortunately, Logan not only made the team the next season, but he was named team captain and proceeded to lead the team to a provincial championship. Logan led the league in goals, assists and points and was named Most Valuable Player of the entire league in not only the regular season but also in the playoffs and the Alberta Provincial tournament. But even that still wasn't enough for him to be given an opportunity by the National Hockey League.

"Hey, Dad," Logan called as they finished up all of the grading for the day. "Hunter gave me a call this morning."

"Hunter, as in your coach from last season?" asked Jacob.

"Yeah, he offered me a job as assistant coach for the Midget AAA team next season," Logan replied.

"Oh, wow, and what did you tell him?"

"Well, I haven't decided yet, but I said I would think about it and get back to him. What do you think I should do?"

"Well, it's not up to me," replied Jacob. "The decision is all yours, but it would be nice to have you stay home and stay involved in hockey at the same time, if that's what you wanted."

"Honestly, I don't even know what I want anymore," Logan admitted as he and Jacob walked along the dirt path towards the house.

Throughout the evening and into the wee hours of the night, Logan contemplated Hunter's offer. He wanted to make his decision sooner rather than later so he wouldn't leave Hunter in a sticky situation. The only that kept Logan from calling Hunter back right away and accepting his offer—aside from the fact that it was about midnight—was that he was having trouble coming to terms with, for all intents and purposes, giving up his lifelong desire to become a professional hockey player.

I guess all kids have to give up their dreams at one point or another, Logan thought.

Logan decided he would call Hunter after work tomorrow to accept his offer. He was going to become the assistant coach of the same team he'd played for the preceding three seasons… and much to his astonishment, Logan didn't mind the sound of that.

Chapter 5

Logan woke up the next morning with the sun shining brightly in his face. The beautiful weather seemed appropriate, considering Logan was about to make the call to start a new era in his life. But before he did, he would go through his morning routine of a shower, a shave, and of course the consumption of the treasured bagels and cream cheese, followed by a day on the job. Logan hopped out of the shower, dressed, and made his way down to the kitchen. Jacob was already sitting at the table reading the newspaper and eating his enormous breakfast of a banana, a pastry, and a cup of coffee. Logan exchanged pleasantries with his father as he opened the fridge to grab the cream cheese. This time, much to Logan's delight, he was not interrupted by his Backstreet Boys ring-tone as he prepared his bagels.

"So, have you made a decision yet?" Jacob asked.

"Yup, I'm gonna call Hunter and accept the offer once we get back tonight—if that's alright with you," Logan added before his father had a chance to swallow the remains of his pastry.

"It's fine with me as long as you're happy."

"Well, I guess we'll find out soon if I'll be happy, won't we?" Logan answered as he finished his second bagel and strolled down the hall towards his bedroom.

Since yesterday had been a grading day, today was a delivery day for Jacob and Logan. They would deliver their eggs to restaurants and grocery stores all over town, and it was far more than just a leisurely drive around town. Once they arrived at each of the restaurants or grocery stores, the two of them would have to unload all the boxes of eggs from the van and carry them inside. From that point, they would move on to their following destination. Just like the grading, it was a fairly uncomplicated process, but it was also tiresome and physically demanding.

When Jacob and Logan finally arrived home at the end of their long day, Logan refused to delay any longer before he called Hunter to accept his offer. But as Logan picked up his cell phone, the line "Backstreet's back alright!" sounded from its speakers before he had the chance to punch in Hunter's phone number.

"Hi, is this Logan Watt?" asked a voice. It sounded somewhat familiar to Logan.

"Yes?"

"Hi, Logan. This is Sean Townsend, the Assistant General Manager of the Vancouver Canucks." Then Logan remembered hearing several interviews with Sean on the radio.

"Mr. Townsend, a pleasure to hear from you," said Logan.

"Well, I can tell you now that you almost heard from me a couple weeks ago," Sean answered, referring to the National Hockey League Entry Draft. "Our scouts are very fond of you, and they had some inside knowledge that no one else would pick you, so we felt it would be in the best interest of our team to offer you a tryout in the summer rather than use our pick on you. So that's what I'm doing right now."

A whirl of thoughts rushed through Logan's mind all at once, and for a few moments he couldn't move or speak. Logan had no idea the Vancouver Canucks had been scouting him, and he certainly had no idea that they were very fond of him.

I thought scouts usually interview the player who they're looking at, or at least let them know they are being scouted. Did Sean Townsend just offer me a spot on the Vancouver Canucks? No, only a tryout. I still have to tryout to make the team, Logan thought. *But I'm a Flames fan; I hate the Canucks.*

Then he reassured himself: *Oh, but would I ever love them if I actually was a Canuck. I think their slogan is 'We are all Canucks,' so maybe I'm already a Canuck?*

"Logan, are you there?" asked Sean after the long, awkward pause.

"Uhh, yeah, sorry," Logan said as he attempted to gather his thoughts and muster up a response. "I would love to tryout with the Vancouver Canucks—it truly would be a dream come true."

"Perfect," said Sean enthusiastically.

"So it's a week-long tryout that starts in two days—sorry for the short notice. We will book your flight immediately and e-mail you everything you need to know within the next few hours. Don't worry about any of the expenses; we'll cover everything. And by everything, I mean everything from air-fare to food."

"Wow, uhh, thanks a lot," Logan said.

"Don't mention it; you're in the big leagues, at least for the next week, so get used to it. And if you don't receive this type of treatment from everyone in our organization, you come to me," Sean finished with a tone of authority.

"Uhh, sounds good," Logan answered, still having trouble coming up with more than three words at a time.

"Perfect, just give me a call at this number if you need anything at all," Sean said as his voice shifted back to its original pleasant tone. "We'll see you soon," he added as he hung up the phone.

A few minutes later, Logan was finally able to let the initial wave of shock and excitement pass as he began to process all this new information. He'd been given a second chance to fulfill his childhood dream, and no matter what the result, he would be forever grateful to Sean Townsend and the entire Vancouver Canucks organization for giving him that second chance. Logan knew that in this day and age second chances were very hard to come by, so he wanted to make the most of the opportunity that was just presented to him.

Logan decided he would try to get some of his friends and old teammates together for a recreational session of stick and puck so he could once again get a feel for the ice before heading to Vancouver for the tryout. But prior to that, Logan had some other things he had to take care of. First of all, he had to call Hunter back and let him know he'd have to delay his response about the coaching offer. And secondly, Logan would have to talk to his father about the tryout and make sure it was alright with him to take a brief leave from the farm. Logan was positive they would both be one hundred percent supportive of his decision, but at the same time, he still felt like he was letting them both down in different ways. However, for the

The Hockey Farmer

first time in his life, with his career on the line, Logan had to put his needs ahead of those of anyone else.

"Hey, Hunter," Logan said as he called to break the news.

"Logan, I've been looking forward to your call. I assume you've come to a decision?" asked Hunter.

"Well, not exactly. My intention was to call you today and let you know I have accepted your offer, but—"

"You changed your mind," Hunter interrupted Logan.

"No, not at all, it's just that I got a tryout offer with the Vancouver Canucks earlier today, and if I made the team—"

"I completely understand," Hunter interrupted Logan a second time. "This is a once in a lifetime opportunity for you. I know you've been working your whole life to become a professional hockey player, and I wouldn't want to stand in your way."

"Thanks, Coach, I really appreciate it."

"Not a problem. If you make the team, we'll support you completely. And if you don't, you know you have a job waiting for you right here with us."

"Thanks again, Coach."

"Good luck, Logan. I'm rooting for ya."

"That wasn't so bad," Logan said under his breath as he hung up the phone.

One down and one to go, he thought.

However, the next item on his list couldn't be done over the phone. It was a face-to-face talk with his father, and for some reason, Logan dreaded the conversation. But he soon decided there was absolutely no point in stressing it; if he had learned anything this summer on the farm, it was to confront his problems dead-on and with full steam. And that was what he was going to do, even if this situation really wasn't exactly a problem.

"Dad, I need to talk to you," Logan said as he helped set the dinner table.

"Sure son, what can I do for you?" Jacob asked, shuffling through the cupboards looking for his special wineglass.

"Sean Townsend, the assistant General Manager of the Vancouver Canucks, called me today and offered me a tryout with the team." Logan wasted no time getting to the point.

"That's fantastic," Jacob said passionately and, it seemed, genuinely. "When do you leave?" he added.

"In two days. They should be e-mailing me with the flight info and all the rest of the details any minute now. They're covering all the expenses, too, so we don't even need to spend a penny."

"Well the news just keeps on getting better," Jacob said with a big smile on his face. "Don't worry about the farm—we'll be fine without you," he added.

"Well, I'll only be away for a week, so just make sure you don't mess things up too much until I get back." Logan spoke with a rare tone of sarcasm as he and his father sat down for a home-cooked meal of the Jacob Watt special: Traditional "sunny-side up" fried eggs covered in Frank's Red Hot Sauce.

Chapter 6

The next day, Logan had big plans and had no time for errors or miscalculations. He spent the first half of the day working on the farm for the last time before he made the trip to Vancouver; this was the closest he would get to a day off all summer. Jacob and Logan had finished delivering the eggs the day before, and the produce company expected them to take two days, so all in all, there was no grading or delivering left to do. Yet Logan attended to all of his other tasks and responsibilities so his father wouldn't have to radically increase his workload while Logan was away. He would farm the tractors, clean everything, and make sure all the barns were in premium shape, and then check the waters. Luckily for Logan, he had finished all the fencing earlier in the summer, so at least he could cross one duty off of his farming check list.

After Logan had taken care of all his responsibilities, he made his way down to the Cochrane Ice Rink. Logan had gotten a group of his hockey friends and old teammates to pitch in ten dollars each so he could rent the rink for a game of pick-up hockey. When Logan arrived at the arena, he was surprised to see one of his oldest friends in the dressing room lacing up his Bauer Vapor skates: Mark Simpson, who'd been drafted by the Toronto Maple Leafs. Logan hadn't known Mark was making a visit to Cochrane, so he was tremendously surprised when he saw his only National Hockey League friend preparing to hit the ice.

"How come I didn't get an invite?" Mark asked light-heartedly when he saw Logan enter the dressing room with his miniscule yet proficient hockey bag.

"Well, I didn't think a hotshot like you would have made the trip down to the old rink since you're now in the show," Logan said sarcastically but with a smile on his face. "How are you doing?" he added.

"Never been better, despite the fact that I'm a Maple Leaf," Mark said as he and Logan both laughed.

It was an inside joke between the two of them. Growing up in Cochrane, Mark and Logan were both huge Calgary Flames fans, and consequently they both despised the Toronto Maple Leafs, the Vancouver Canucks, and of course the Edmonton Oilers with a passion. It had never once crossed Mark's mind that he might eventually become a member of the team he always loved to hate.

"Hey, if I were in your shoes, I wouldn't be complaining!" Logan said as he took a seat next to Mark on the bench and began to put on his equipment.

"I know, eh... who am I kidding? The Leafs are my favourite team now for sure."

"I pity you," Logan shot back, and they shared another round of laughter. "At least you know you'll be playing in front of a packed house every night," he added.

"That's what I was thinking. You can say whatever you want about the Maple Leafs and their fans, but they know their stuff and they love their hockey," said Mark. "Speaking of which, I heard Vancouver is a hockey-crazed city in itself, and rumour is that you're on your way to the big city."

"Yeah, I'm heading out tomorrow afternoon for a week-long tryout, so I guess if they like what they see from me, they'll keep me around. And if not, I think I'm going to take up Hunter's offer to help coach the Midget team."

"I wouldn't worry about that," Mark answered. "I'm surprised you didn't get drafted, but I'm sure they'll keep you in the fold once you strut your stuff at the tryout."

"Man, I hope so. This could be my last chance to make it to the show just like you, big guy."

"Well, I'm not quite there yet—I still have to make the team," Mark replied. "But the Canucks, eh—boy do I ever pity you," he added as they strapped on their helmets and made their way down the hall to the rink.

When Logan and Mark made their way onto the ice, they were caught off-guard by a relatively loud cheer from spectators. Well, loud for the Cochrane arena, though not in comparison to a state of the art National Hockey League building like the Air Canada Center in Toronto or General Motors Place in Vancouver. Apparently, rumours had swirled around that Mark Simpson, the new pride of Cochrane, Alberta, was back in town and would be signing autographs after his the pick-up game at the Cochrane Arena. This was the first Mark heard of the signing autographs bit, but he didn't mind; he was actually somewhat flattered.

As the game got rolling, more and more people started to arrive, most to catch a glimpse of Mark Simpson. However, much to his surprise, some also came to watch Logan. He even saw a "Good Luck in Vancouver, Logan" sign in the crowd. Logan didn't know how the word got out so quickly, but just like Mark, he was somewhat flattered.

It wasn't much of an entertaining game; it had the intensity identical to that of a National Hockey League All-Star game. They were all friends, and no one wanted to risk getting an injury in this friendly game, so there was an apparent lack of interest and intensity at times. However, it became a little more exciting towards the end of the game as the competitive nature of the boys took over. Logan and Mark were on opposite teams, and Logan felt as though he had something to prove by going head to head against Mark, if only to himself. He knew playing against Mark would be a good test and preparation for what was to come at the Canucks tryout. Off the ice, they were the best of friends, but on it, they were two soldiers doing battle against one another—and it began to show when Logan and Mark went into the corner together looking for the puck. They bumped shoulders and both lost their balance; however, neither lost his footing. They proceeded to battle in the corner for the puck until the final buzzer went off.

The final buzzer marked the end of the game, but not the end of their miniature altercation. Mark wasn't happy with the way Logan had initiated contact as they'd entered the corner, and he let him know about it. Logan didn't back down. Cooler heads prevailed, but not for long. They at last decided to move their impassioned discussion into the dressing room, behind closed doors and out of the public eye.

"What was that all about?" yelled Mark as he threw his stick onto the rack and ripped his helmed off for emphasis.

The Hockey Farmer

"I was just playing hard," Logan said calmly as he placed his stick on the rack and took a seat on the bench in the dressing room.

"You don't body check in a game like this; it isn't the Stanley Cup Finals, Watter," said Mark, evidently still pissed off.

"It wasn't a body check, Simpson. We bumped into each other," Logan countered, as cool as a cucumber. "Don't sweat it, man," he added.

"I have to go sign them autographs." Mark packed up his equipment and left the dressing room without saying another word to Logan or anyone else.

Logan thought Mark was harshly overreacting; he didn't know why Mark was making such a big deal out of a little bump in the corner. Even though Logan and Mark had been the best of friends growing up, this sort of disagreement wasn't unusual for them. During their second year of Pee Wee, Logan and Mark almost dropped gloves during a practice even though they were on the same team. However, that wasn't the last of their disputes related to hockey. During their first year of Midget, Logan and Mark did indeed drop gloves during an intra-squad game in the rep tryouts, and Logan got a bloody nose to show for it.

Logan quickly stored away his equipment and subsequently made his way to the lobby of the arena. As Logan watched Mark signing autographs, he wanted to patch up all their differences before he left for Vancouver. Unfortunately, it didn't look like the autograph session was going to end any time soon—it actually appeared as though the line-up was mounting—and Logan had to get home to pack. His customary post-confrontation discussion with Mark would have to wait.

Chapter 7

"Last call for all passengers for flight 327 to Vancouver, British Columbia," the monotone P.A. announcer in the airport reported three times before Logan finally arrived to the correct gate.

Logan wasn't familiar with the Calgary airport or the process of flying in general, since he had only been on an airplane once. And since that trip had been back when Logan was merely a child, it took him much longer than he'd expected to find the right gate and board his plane to beautiful British Columbia.

When Logan arrived a few hours later at the airport in Vancouver, it took him much longer than it should have to find all his baggage and equipment, but in due time— and with the assistance of an airport employee—he made it happen. In his e-mail, Sean had said someone would be waiting outside the airport to give Logan a ride directly to the hotel where all the other players were staying. Logan accordingly made his way outside and saw someone standing right next to a black limo, holding up a sign with his name on it.

"You gotta be kidding me," Logan thought to himself, delighted, as he walked towards the man with the sign.

The Hockey Farmer

"Are you Logan Watt?" asked the man in a custom tailored pinstriped black suit.

"Sure am," responded Logan.

"Nice to meet you. Hop in and I'll take you to the hotel—most of the other players are already there."

"Yes, sir," Logan said as he entered the limo with no hesitance whatsoever.

Logan hadn't seen very many limos growing up in Cochrane, a small town in comparison to Calgary and Vancouver, but whenever he had, he'd always tried to catch a glimpse of whoever was inside to see if it was a celebrity he recognized. As they drove from one side of the city to the other, Logan saw himself in many young children who were trying to do the same. At one red light, he was even tempted to slide open the window and let the children know he was no celebrity, only a normal teenage kid. Logan didn't arrive at the hotel until about two hours later. The airport was in Richmond, a suburb of Vancouver, and the hotel was right in the heart of downtown, so Logan sat in the limo for much longer than he would have expected—but he certainly wasn't about to start complaining.

"Well, here we are," said the driver. "The Fairmont Hotel Vancouver, one of the best places in town to stay."

"Thanks for the ride," Logan answered.

"Good luck, kid," replied the driver before he drove back into the mayhem of downtown Vancouver.

Logan went to the front desk to check in and figure out which of the five hundred rooms in this five-star hotel was his for the keeping, at least for the week. The hotel clerk informed him that all the other players were currently in the Griffins Restaurant, if he wanted to go and meet them. Logan decided to go to his third-floor room first and freshen up a bit before he joined the team for dinner.

About twenty minutes later, Logan was making his way down to the restaurant when he saw a group of teenagers enter the lobby. And they weren't just any teenagers. Logan knew a group of hockey players when he saw them.

"These must be the guys I'm going up against," Logan said under his breath.

"They certainly are," said a man with a somewhat sinister, smug look who crept up out of nowhere. "I'm Aaron Vixen, your potential Head Coach," the man added.

"Ah, of course, a pleasure to meet you," Logan answered. "I was just about to join you guys in the restaurant, but I see you're obviously done eating now."

"Oh don't worry about it; I just went up to your room to drag you down here and introduce you to the guys anyway. I guess we just missed each other," Aaron answered. "But you're here now, so let's go introduce you to everyone."

"Sounds good. Lead the way," Logan said as he followed Aaron to the hotel reception area.

Logan was pleasantly surprised when he started talking to some of the other players and found that this was unfamiliar waters for a lot of them, too. Logan had thought he would arrive in Vancouver and be the outsider of the group, but he soon realized they were all going through the same thing, and that helped Logan feel a lot more comfortable and relaxed. Logan was also pleasantly surprised by how friendly all the guys were, though he didn't want to read too much into their off-ice personalities. Due to his past experiences with Mark, Logan knew that once you're on the ice fighting for a job, everything changes. But then again, he was going to enjoy the few days he had with the group before they went to battle on the ice.

"Wait until you check out the broads in this city," said Scott Bell, one of the other players as they sat in one of the conference rooms waiting for the Assistant Coach to address the team. "Tell them you play for the Canucks, and you can basically pick and choose which girl you want in Van City, especially with your rugged look."

Logan chuckled.

"We'll take you out to a big party after the week is over; hopefully we'll have something to celebrate. How long are you in town for?" Scott asked.

"Umm, I'm not exactly sure when they booked my return flight, but I'm assuming I'll be heading back the day after tryouts."

"Alright, well let me know. I've lived in this city my whole life, so I know all the ins and outs, if you know what I mean," Scott said.

"Is this your first tryout with the Canucks?" asked Logan.

"Nah, man, I was here last year, was one of the last cuts," Scott answered.

"Ouch, that's gotta hurt."

"If there's any advice I could give you, it's watch out for Luke Brown—he's not here yet, but that guy is trouble on and off the ice. He'll try to hurt you on the ice, and he will try to get on your nerves off it," Scott added as the Assistant Coach made his way into the conference room.

Logan thought about what Scott had said as the Assistant Coach talked to one of the hotel employees before making his speech to the team—and he wasn't the least bit intimidated. Logan was always one of the smaller players, and he was used to others targeting him on the ice, so he wasn't exactly shaking in his boots when he heard about Luke. And if Logan worried too much about the other players and what they were doing, he wouldn't be able to properly focus on his performance and making a positive impression on the coaching staff. Logan knew that if he paid too much attention to Luke Brown—or any other player, for that matter—he would be playing right into their hands.

It turned out the Assistant Coach really didn't give much of a speech. He introduced himself along with some of the other members of the Canucks staff, then went over the schedule for the rest of the week along with his expectations, both behavioural and performance-wise. He said the next morning would be fitness testing followed by a full day of sightseeing and team bonding all over the city. The fitness testing in these types of tryouts was physically demanding, to say the least. Most players absolutely dreaded it.

Logan was also very excited to actually get out and see Vancouver up close. He had heard how beautiful Vancouver was but had never experienced it for himself, aside from looking out his window on the ride from the airport.

"That's about it," said the Assistant Coach as he wrapped up his address to the team.

"What about curfew?" yelled Scott from the back of the room.

The Hockey Farmer

"Do whatever you want, go wherever you want, get back to the hotel whenever you want, but don't be late for any team functions or ice times," he said.

A wave of chatter and excitement took over the room. To Logan, it seemed as though most of the players were more excited about going out and partying than focusing on hockey, which was completely fine by him. This would only increase his chances of accomplishing the goal he'd made for the trip to Vancouver for. Logan wasn't here to try and ameliorate his social life, he only had one goal in mind: To earn a contract with the Vancouver Canucks.

"We're not here to babysit you. If you want to go out all night and get hammered, that's your call, but don't expect any leniency from us," added the Assistant Coach.

"Big party tonight downtown, who's down?" Scott said sarcastically, and the team shared some laughter.

"Our job is to run the drills on the ice and determine which of you are ready to make the next step, and that's it. Everything else is on all of your individual shoulders," said Head Coach Aaron Vixen, who hadn't spoken for the entire meeting until that point. "So with that said, we'll see you all tomorrow in the gym at seven-thirty—don't be late."

When Logan went back up to his room, he felt much more comfortable and less stressed than he had the night before. He now knew most of the players and coaches were great people, very welcoming and fun to be around. Logan wasn't looking forward to waking up early and being tested by the team trainers, but he was ready to make a positive impression on the coaches during the fitness testing, even though it was no more than a formality. He was also aware that the dreaded Luke Brown would be joining the team at testing tomorrow morning—but unlike a lot of the other players, Logan was rather interested to meet him. Throughout the day, several of the players had warned Logan not to antagonize Luke because he was the true definition of a "nut job." Although Logan wasn't planning on provoking anyone, he wasn't going to fear or completely avoid the apparent "nut case" either. Logan went to sleep that night itching to wake up the next morning to get the fitness testing over with, enjoy a day of sightseeing in the city, and then finally set foot on the ice and start his ultimate quest to play in the National Hockey League.

Chapter 8

Even though Logan had the hotel's alarm clock and his phone alarm set for six-thirty to give him enough time to shower and get some food into his system before the fitness testing, neither of them woke him up. At six-fifteen, Logan received a wake-up call from the hotel front desk, even though he hadn't set one up the previous night. The woman on the phone said this was the first and last time the coaching staff would set up a wake-up call for each of the players.

I thought they weren't here to baby-sit us. Logan jumped out of his bed and made his way to the luxurious bathroom. Despite his countless early morning hockey practices as a child and the many times Logan had to wake up this early to help his father work on the farm, he still wasn't much of an early bird. It usually took Logan a couple hours after he woke up to start functioning at one hundred percent, but today he was determined to end that potentially costly trend. He had to or else he would regret it for the rest of his life.

When Logan arrived at the gym around seven-fifteen, only a couple of the trainers and four or five players were there. But as the time crept closer to seven-thirty, more and more players and staff began to arrive in the training facility of The Fairmont Hotel. Logan was uneasy and a little nervous, but he knew the nerves would go away once he actually started doing something besides sitting around waiting for the festivities to get under way. After all the routine blood samples had been taken, the players branched off into several different sections of the training facility. Section one was push-ups and sit-ups, section two was aerobic testing on the bike, section three was weight lifting and bench press, and section four was the vertical jump and balance test section, perhaps the easiest of the groups.

Logan was pleased to start off in section two, as he'd predicted that aerobics and endurance would be his strongest area—and he was right. Logan definitely started the day of fitness testing off on the right foot, figuratively and literally speaking. He blew the trainers away and caught the attention of several other players with his above-average leg strength and stamina on the stationary bike. He also put on a very good show in the sprint portion of the endurance testing. Logan had always paid close attention to leg strength to make up for his lack of size, and this was evident in his performance on the bike.

From there he moved on to the next station, the weight lifting and bench press, which Logan thought would be his weak link. Unlike the first section, Logan didn't blow anyone away with his performance on the weights. However, he was right around the average results of the rest of the players.

Halfway through his testing, Logan made his way to the least physically demanding of the stations: The vertical jump and balance test section. Logan once again stole the show, as he seemed well at ease balancing his entire body on the apparatus. He also put on a spectacular display in the vertical jump portion—his best out of three verticals was recorded at 28 inches, which could be attributed to the two years he played on his high school basketball team. Logan's last station for the day was the push-ups and sit-ups section. The players were required to do one minute of push-ups followed immediately by one minute of sit-ups, repeated three times for a grand total of six straight minutes of cardiovascular activity. Logan didn't begin struggling and slowing down his pace until the fourth minute, which was about the median for the day. However, he stuck it out and was able to complete the entire six minutes of push-ups and sit-ups without any overly extended pauses. As another plus, Logan was one of a select group of players who did not require a bucket after the push-ups and sit-ups.

"The trainers tell me you had some great results in the testing today," said Coach Aaron Vixen as Logan took a breather and watched some of the others finish up in the training facility.

"Well..." Logan paused, desperately in need of oxygen, as he continued to sweat profusely and breathe heavily. "I definitely tried my hardest," he was able to get out as he tried not to look too worn-out in front of Coach Vixen, the person who would ultimately decide his fate with the Canucks.

"And that's all we ask of you guys," Coach said. "The above-average fitness results are no more than a bonus; however, if you can't back up your results in the training room with above-average performance once we hit the ice, then you have a problem," added Coach Vixen.

"I completely understand," Logan said, realizing Coach Vixen was testing his mental abilities and judgement while he was tired. "I can't wait to get on the ice and show you what I can really do," he added, still gasping for air, yet somehow finding a way to speak normally.

"And we can't wait to see you on the ice. Our scouts are pretty high on you, kid, so we'll be keeping a close eye on you, but all we want you to do is play your game. We don't want you to go out of your comfort zone and try to do something special," Coach Vixen said.

"I understand," Logan answered, itching to end the conversation so he could make his way back to his room and hop into the shower.

"Alright, well go clean yourself up, get some food into your system, get some rest, and we'll give you a shout in a couple hours when we head out for the sightseeing trip," said Coach Vixen, also eager to end the discussion and go talk to some of the other players.

"Sounds good," Logan said as he exited the training facility and made his way back up to his room.

Logan had actually completely forgotten about the sightseeing trip. After the early morning fitness testing, the only three things in Logan's mind were exactly what Coach Vixen had said: Food, shower, and sleep. He wasn't as excited about the day in the city anymore; still, it would be a good way to spend some time with the boys in a relaxing setting before they started the actual hockey portion of the tryout the next morning. Also, this would be his only free time all week to actually get out and see what the city was all about.

After Logan had a shower, he wasn't too keen on leaving the room again until the trip later in the afternoon, so he didn't. Logan put up the "do not disturb" sign on the outside of his door, hopped onto his bed, grabbed the remote and switched on the television, and then made a call to the Fairmont Hotel Vancouver's restaurant to order some lunch.

Now this is the life, he thought.

Chapter 9

Much to his dismay, Logan's nap was interrupted with another call from the front desk.

"The bus is here. Come down to the lobby—we're leaving in 15 minutes," said one of the several Canucks Coaches who were swarming around the Fairmont Hotel Vancouver.

"I'm on my way." Logan hung up the phone and jumped out of bed, feeling completely recharged and rejuvenated after his meal and power nap.

Logan grabbed his cell phone and wallet from the bedside table, put on some jogging pants, snatched his Reebok hoodie and hat lying side by side on the sofa, and made his way down to the lobby.

"Hold the elevator," yelled a muscular man in his early twenties.

The man's face seemed much too familiar to Logan. He thought about where he had seen him before as he held open the elevator door and waited for the man to come in. *I saw this guy in the training facility this morning*, Logan realized as the man entered the elevator. *He took part in all of the testing, but I didn't see him yesterday at the team dinner or meeting.*

It couldn't be Luke Br—, thought Logan as the man interrupted him.

The Hockey Farmer

"Luke Brown," the man introduced himself. "I saw you this morning. You trying out for the Nucks?"

"Uhh, yeah, are you?" Logan asked, acting as if he'd never heard the name Luke Brown.

"Sure am," answered Luke.

This guy doesn't seem too bad, Logan thought.

"Well, you better watch out, kid—this is my territory, and I don't take anything from anyone, you got that?" Luke said with an evil-looking smile. "Oh, and I hate rookies," he added.

"Uhh, okay," Logan answered as his opinion of the dreaded Luke Brown immediately changed.

"Good luck," Luke said sarcastically as the elevator door opened and he made his way to the lobby.

"What a tool," Logan muttered under his breath as he followed Luke.

The team's first stop was Science World at the Telus World of Science. The attraction – formally known as just Science World - featured many interactive exhibits and displays as well as areas with varying topics throughout the years. For players such as Scott Bell, who were from around the lower mainland area, they weren't too interested in the center—they had already been there and seen what it had to offer on numerous occasions. But Logan had never seen anything like Science World. He was in awe just looking at its rounded shape from the outside before they had even entered the building. It was a really spectacular sight to see. Once they stepped inside, the group of guys received more than a few curious looks, and they were almost immediately swarmed by a group of children looking for autographs. Logan and the rest of the players sat in the lobby signing autographs for about half an hour before they actually went on their tour around Science World. Then they finished off their visit with a movie at the OMNIMAX Theatre.

From there, the group made a stop at the renowned Granville Island, which lies right in the center of Vancouver. It was jam-packed with restaurants, theatres, galleries, and studios occupied by both artists and craftspeople. It was also the place to go for fresh food, clothes, gifts, crafts, and free street entertainment or a drink and a snack in the sun overlooking False Creek. The team split up into two groups and wandered off on their own around the island for about an hour before they had to meet up and hop on the bus for the next stop of the day. Even though Logan told himself he wouldn't be intimidated by Luke Brown, he was somewhat relieved that Luke was not in his group. During the hour, Logan's group did a little bit of everything while Luke's group visited the Granville Island Brewing Company and took the tour that ended with a sampling of the brews in their private bar. Logan was awed by Vancouver's beauty and by how different the lifestyle was compared to that of Cochrane.

Next on the list of tourist attractions was the Capilano Suspension Bridge. This site was another "must-see" in Vancouver, as well as the group's first voyage out of the downtown area. The suspension bridge was located in North Vancouver, fairly close to Horseshoe Bay, the port for the BC ferries. The bridge, which swung and twisted 230 feet above the rocks and surf below, was a grand total of 450 feet long—so it wasn't just "a walk in the park." Logan was surprised to see Luke Brown, supposedly the toughest and most fearless player on the team, clinging to the ropes and not looking down below as he crossed the

The Hockey Farmer

bridge. Luke almost had a nervous breakdown when some of the others bounced up and down in the middle, trying to make the bridge swing faster to get on his nerves. Logan couldn't help to share a chuckle or two with his teammates when he saw Luke in this state of mind.

Lastly, the team had the option to visit the Vancouver Aquarium. However, a lot of the guys were feeling worn out after the morning fitness testing followed by a day walking around the city. So they had a vote, and the majority of the players decided to call it a day and head back to the hotel. Even though Logan really wanted to check out the Vancouver Aquarium and all of its animals, he too voted to return to the hotel—he felt it would serve him better to get as much rest as possible before the next day's on-ice session.

When the team finally returned to the Fairmont Hotel, each of the players had another hour to freshen up before their team dinner, followed by another team meeting in the conference room to outline the schedule for the next day. As Logan entered the elevator to go up to his room, he heard the same unwelcome voice from earlier in the day.

"Hold the door," yelled Luke Brown, for the second time that day.

Logan complied with Luke's wishes; however, this time around Luke didn't say anything to Logan. He was in all likelihood too embarrassed about what had happened at the Capilano Suspension Bridge. Logan was tempted to rub Luke's fear of heights in his face but thought better of it.

"Is this your first year with the team?" asked Logan, trying to make conversation and put an end to the awkward silence in the elevator.

"Are you kidding me?" Luke answered. "Does it look like this is my first year?
No, it doesn't, because it's not, ya rook. And who gives you, a frickin rookie from Alberta, the right to talk to me on my turf?"

Logan was actually somewhat flattered that Luke knew he was from Alberta, and he wondered if he was supposed to answer that question. Luke was obviously frustrated with the earlier incident at the bridge and was taking out all of his anger on Logan. While he didn't want to antagonize Luke, Logan wasn't about to get walked all over either.

"So it's not your first year, but you still haven't made the team?" Logan asked rhetorically. "Wow, that's rough," he went on before Luke had a chance to respond.

Luke seemed rather stunned by Logan's comments. No one had ever had the guts to talk to him that way, and for that reason, Luke was completely silent until the elevator finally arrived on his floor.

"Watch yourself tomorrow, kid. I've injured at least one player at each of the tryouts I've been to, and I don't expect that trend to stop this year, bud," Luke threatened as he left the elevator.

What a tool, Logan thought again as he watched Luke strut down the hall, acting as if he owned the whole world.

Nothing too eventful happened at the team dinner or meeting aside from Scott Bell, the team clown, making a fool of himself on more than one occasion. Every team had a Scott Bell type of character in the dressing room, someone who was ultimately needed to provide comic relief during tense times and to raise the team's spirits during the rough rides. During the team meeting, the Assistant Coach went over the schedule for the real first day of tryouts. He split the team up into two different groups. Group one would go on the ice first thing in the morning and then have their dry-land training afterwards, while group two would do the opposite. Logan was in group two, and much to his despair, Luke Brown would be joining him.

Chapter 10

Logan's alarm clock went off at six-fifteen the next morning, and he still felt somewhat drained from the fitness testing and sightseeing the day before. He wanted to just pretend he'd never heard the alarm clock, roll over, and go back to bed. However, Logan knew if he was late to report this morning, he would be asking for his death bed. As Logan willed himself out of bed five minutes later, making his way to the bathroom, he noticed his phone was flashing. He had two new text messages.

"Good luck today. The farm is still rolling along quite nicely," said the first message, from Jacob.

Logan couldn't help having a little chuckle as he read his father's message. He remembered how long it took him to teach his father how to text message; at least his efforts hadn't gone to waste.

"Good luck 2day boy, we all rootin for ya back home. Oh, and sry about what happened at the arena, it was my turn wasnt it?" said the second message, from Mark.

For a second time with his phone in hand, Logan had a chuckle. Firstly, he found it comical that Mark texted in slang while in person he was one of the most well-spoken people Logan knew. Secondly, Logan had known he'd receive an apology message from Mark sooner rather than later. Whenever they got into an altercation, one of them always took initiative and sent an apology message. They would alternate every time, and Logan knew he had sent the last message a few years back, so he was already expecting one from Mark.

Logan made his way down to the lobby around seven-fifteen, after he had showered and had a quick bite of nothing other than bagels and cream cheese. The bus to General Motors Place was scheduled to leave at seven-thirty, so that left fifteen minutes of downtime for Logan before he would "go to war," as Hunter—Logan's former coach—always used to say before a game. General Motors Place was right across the street from Science World, so Logan had already seen it from the outside. As more players and staff members trickled into the lobby minute by minute, Logan realized this was what he'd been waiting for his whole life. He was less than a couple hours away from donning a National Hockey League jersey, even though it was merely a practice jersey.

Logan had never been inside General Motors Place, but he'd seen it on his television whenever he watched the Calgary Flames play against the Canucks—which was quite often, since the two teams were Northwest Division rivals. Much to Logan's disappointment, when he stepped foot inside, there wasn't much time to look around and examine the state of the facility. Group one, including Scott Bell, was immediately ushered by an arena employee to the dressing rooms to get prepared for their on-ice session. Meanwhile, group two, including Logan and Luke, was ushered to the General Motors Place training facility, which was pretty much connected to the dressing rooms, to commence their dry-land training. Logan wished he could have watched the first group's on-ice session instead of working out so he would know what to expect, but that was not an option.

"Alright, all of you listen up. Get on the bike for twenty minutes non-stop; we'll be monitoring your speed. Then we'll bring in the yoga instructor so you guys can properly stretch for another twenty minutes before it's your turn on the ice," said Mike Barnstable, the team's head athletic trainer. "We don't want any injuries here on the first day, now do we," he added as Logan and the others found unoccupied stationary bikes and got under way.

As Logan and the rest of the group hit the ten-minute mark on the bike, he wondered what it would be like doing yoga. *Do hockey players really do this type of stuff?* he wondered.

The fact of the matter was that hockey players did do yoga—for one, just like Mike Barnstable said; it was a great way to prevent injury by stretching all the necessary muscles. But in addition, Mike later informed the group that they had a sort of advantage over group one because doing yoga right before their on-ice session would relax their muscles and their mind, ultimately improving their performance on the ice.

When the twenty minutes of bike riding were over, Logan made his way down the hall to grab a bottle of water. As he picked up a bottle from the package in the hallway, he saw one of the players behind him entering the dressing room, heavily labouring and favouring his right shoulder. Logan decided to take a sneak peak and realized this wasn't just any player—it was Scott Bell.

"Scott, what happened, man?" Logan asked with sincere concern.

"Ah, we were doing the gauntlet, man; I blew out my shoulder," Scott answered, obviously still in a hefty amount of pain.

The gauntlet was a drill where all players on the ice except one lined up about one meter away from the boards, and then the other player would skate in between the boards and the line of players as fast as he could, trying to avoid the body checks of each and every player in the line. It wasn't hard for Logan to figure out that one of the players had obviously made solid contact with Scott, and his shoulder had in all likelihood been smashed into the boards.

"Did the doctor check it out?" Logan asked.

"Yeah, he looked at it quickly and told me to wait in here," Scott responded, grimacing in pain.

"Did he say anything?"

"No, man, but I could tell from his face that it didn't look good. Every year, something stupid happens that stops me from making this team. I really thought this would be the year I made it." Scott ripped off his helmet and threw it across the dressing room.

"I'm sorry, man, hopefully the injury's not too bad, but I gotta get back—" Logan began as Scott interrupted him.

"Yeah, you don't wanna keep anyone waiting. Good luck. Now that I'm out, you actually have a chance to make the team," Scott joked. Logan laughed and left the room.

When Logan rejoined the others in the yoga session, he realized that without even knowing it, he had done yoga in the past. He'd never gone to an actual class or anything of that sort, but Logan realized that he had already done some of the stretches and poses the instructor showed them before games and practices. While the group was in the relaxation pose to finish off the session, Logan told the others the first group had done the gauntlet drill, and Scott Bell had thrown out his shoulder in the process. Logan could see Luke Brown across the room salivating at the opportunity to staple him to the boards during the gauntlet.

"What's the matter, Watt, never done the gauntlet before?" Luke yelled from across the room as the others immediately turned silent.

"I think all hockey players have done it at one time or another," Logan responded calmly.

"Well, I guess what I'm trying to ask is, have you ever done the gauntlet against real men? Even though you're only five feet tall, this isn't Pee Wee anymore, kid. This is the real show." Luke had the same evil smile on his face as he had in the elevator the previous day.

I'm actually 5'9" Logan fumed.

"Well, I guess we'll find out soon enough, won't we?" Logan retorted as the others in the room stared at him, wondering what he was thinking by irritating the ruthless Luke Brown.

It was fairly obvious that Luke Brown chose a different rookie to pick on every year, and Logan was that guy this year. So Logan didn't really take Luke's ill-treatment too personally. But judging by the reaction from all the experienced players who knew what Luke was actually all about, Logan surmised that no one else had ever stood on his own two feet like he was, but instead just rolled over and took the abuse. Logan may have been lacking in size, but he certainly wasn't lacking in courage.

"Alright, that's about it, boys. Start getting ready— you should all be on the ice in no more then twenty-five minutes," said the head athletic trainer, Mike Barnstable. "See you all tomorrow, and good luck," added Mike as he left the room, followed almost instantaneously by the rest of the players.

Logan tried to put all his equipment on as fast as he could—he was always one of the players who took the longest to tie his skates, and he wanted to be one of the first on the ice, just to get a feel for it. Much to Logan's surprise, there wasn't much chatter going on in the dressing room as everyone seemed to be focusing and trying to get into the right mindset to play hockey. So he thought he should probably be doing the same. All he could hear was the strapping of hockey tape as Luke and some others taped their sticks, as well as the loud banter coming from the other dressing room where the players from the first session were changing. Logan felt encouraged as he heard the positive vibe coming from the other dressing room.

They don't sound too worn out; how bad could it be? he thought.

Some of the players started getting up and making their way onto the ice. Logan could tell by the looks of all their faces that the jokes and laid-back attitude from the previous day at the hotel and in the city had transformed into focus and sheer intensity. Logan tightened up his skates for the third and final time, strapped on his helmet, picked up both of his wooden sticks from the rack, said a little prayer, and made his way down the hall.

This is really happening, he thought as he walked down the tunnel, threw his spare stick on the bench, and stepped foot on the ice at General Motors Place for the first time in his life.

Chapter 11

Wow, there's quite a few people here, Logan noticed as he skated lightly around the rink before the tryout actually got started.

General Motors Place was one of the biggest buildings in all of the National Hockey League. It had a capacity of 18,630 spectators, split up into upper and lower bowl sections. Whenever the Vancouver Canucks played a regular season game, every single seat would be sold out; they had something like two hundred consecutive games sold-out. Logan hadn't expected to see many people watching from the stands, seeing as this was merely a prospects camp in the morning during summer break. But almost the entire lower bowl was jam-packed with fans of all ages.

"They love their hockey here in Vancouver," said Coach Aaron Vixen as he noticed Logan gazing into the stands.

"Apparently," Logan answered as he wondered what the others were thinking as they saw him skate around the rink with Coach Vixen.

"The thing is, a lot of our fans can't afford to come out to an actual game because the prices are quite hefty, so this is the closest some of them will ever get," Coach Vixen explained.

"But none of us are actually even on the Canucks," said Logan.

"Yes, but our fans also know their hockey, and they know a few years down the road, a few of you from this group will be playing for us," responded the Coach.

"I guess that makes sense." Logan remembered going to Calgary Flames practices sometimes because his was one of the families that couldn't afford to go to an actual game.

"The key is to just pretend as if no one is watching you, and you'll be fine," Coach Vixen advised. "We better get this show on the road," he added as he skated away towards the assistant coaches, who were at the bench, and blew the whistle.

As Logan skated towards the coaches at the bench with all the other players, Luke came up behind Logan and gave him a little tap on the shoulder.

"So we're sucking up to the coach now, are we?" asked Luke with that smile that, in less than two days, Logan had already become so accustomed to.

"He started talking to me first," Logan answered, not looking to get into another argument.

"Sure, kid. No one likes a teacher's pet, especially not me," said Luke as they both arrived at the bench and joined the huddle forming around the coaches.

"Alright, boys, starting now, we are paying close attention to every single move you make," said Coach Vixen. "Whether it is bad stick position, turning rather than stopping, a lazy back check or a bad pass, we see it all. We have scouts all over the building and some members of the management in the press box as well, so no good or bad move you make will go unnoticed."

"Now with that said, let's get started. Let's get three hard forward laps around the ice followed by three laps around the ice skating backwards. Then stretch it out in the middle as a team," said one of the assistant coaches. "And go!" he yelled as the players got up off their knees and started skating around the rink.

Right away, Logan was aware he was no longer playing amateur hockey in Cochrane. *These guys are going hard*, he thought as he tried to keep up with the group.

Logan was taken aback by the speed and drive of the other players. He found himself watching the others instead of doing what he was supposed to be doing, skating hard. When he played amateur hockey, Logan had always led the pack in these types of skates without even trying. But today he was struggling to stay in the middle of the pack, and he was pushing the pedal to the metal. Skating was supposed to be Logan's strong suit, too.

With my size, if I can't skate, why would they even want to keep me around? Logan wondered as he finished the first three laps and pivoted to switch to backwards skating.

I can't start questioning myself now. I just need time to adjust to the speed and I'll be fine, Logan reassured himself as he blocked out all the other thoughts twirling around in his mind and focused solely on the task at hand.

Once the team collectively finished their stretch at center ice, they made their way back to the benches to grab some water and find out what was next on the list for the day's practice. Coach Vixen informed the group that they would now be doing the full ice Philly drill, which was a common drill for all hockey teams at all levels. Half the players would line up in the right corner at one side of the

The Hockey Farmer

ice, and the others would line up in the left corner at the other side of the ice. One player at a time from each group would then skate along the boards and cut through the middle at the far blue line to receive a pass from the next person in line. After receiving the pass, the player would curl around and shoot on the goaltender on the same side they'd started on. Logan was third in line.

The first player in line was Frank Dempster, who played for his hometown team, the Nanaimo Clippers of the British Columbia Hockey League. The British Columbia League was a step down from the Canadian League but still a higher level of competition than the Cochrane amateur hockey system where Logan came from. After Frank received the pass, he went in and shot bottom left corner and he beat the goalie, but he didn't beat the post. Next was Brent Jackson from the Vancouver Giants of the Western Hockey League. Brent went in and aimed to the top right corner, but the goaltender stuck out his glove and flashed the leather. Then it was Logan's turn; would he be the first of the day to put the puck in the net?

Logan skated as hard as he could down the boards, cut through the middle at the opposite blue line, and received a pass right on the tape from none other than Luke Brown. You could say whatever you wanted about Luke Brown and his attitude problems, but he was a pretty skilled hockey player, and Logan soon realized that.

Wow, that was a good pass, Logan thought as he skated towards the goalie with the puck on his stick, trying to decide whether to shoot or deke.

Logan quickly decided to go with his "bread and butter" deke, which was faking the shot and going to the backhand. He skated into the zone with quite a bit of speed, slowed down once he hit the hash marks, hoping to throw the goalie off with his change in pace. Logan went in and faked the shot, the goalie went down into the butterfly, and Logan made the move to his backhand and lifted the puck top corner. The mesh rippled.

"Nice goal, man," said Brent Jackson as Logan joined him in the line-up. "I love that move."

"Thanks, man; that's pretty much the only move I have," Logan answered as they both laughed quietly.

Logan would only get the opportunity to shoot three more times before Coach Vixen decided it was time to run a different drill. The next time, Logan tried to simply shoot five-hole, but the goalie stopped it—he wasn't about to let in two goals in a row against the rookie. Logan missed the next shot too, but went back to his "bread and butter" deke on his last shot, and it worked again without a hitch. Logan was content with at least two goals out of four shots, which was more than most of the others got.

"The next drill is pretty simple," said Coach Vixen. "All we're going to do is some one-on-ones, so let's get all the defence-men at center ice and all the forwards behind the net."

Logan made his way behind the net. He wondered if he should try to deke through the defence-man or just use his speed and attempt to skate around his opponent and drive to the net. He decided to wait and see which defence-man he was going up against and then make his decision accordingly. Luke Brown was the first defence-man in line and Logan was the second forward in line, so he didn't have to worry about Luke trying anything shady. After Randy Wright—one of the other rookies of the group—was completely tooled by Luke Brown, Logan saw he'd be going up against Brent Jackson. Logan had watched Brent skate during the full ice Philly drill, and he thought his best chance to beat him was to simply take advantage of Brent's lack of mobility by taking him to the outside. So that's what he did.

Logan entered the zone with his head up, coming from the right side. Logan noticed that Brent continued to back up, so he wondered if he should just take a shot but then thought better of it. Logan made a quick move to the inside and saw that Brent had stumbled. Logan then immediately came back to the right and drove to the net. He protected the puck on his backhand with his left foot, then made a quick move back to his forehand. Logan quickly snapped the puck, and it squeaked through the goaltender's legs.

"Damnit!" yelled Brent as the goaltender swept the puck out of the back of his net.

Logan skated back towards the line-up behind the net with no emotion on his face. Logan was a master of the poker face; he didn't want to show the other players or the coaches what was on his mind at any given time. But it wasn't really even a poker face that Logan was putting on, because he was never one for celebrations anyways. The most anyone would get out of him was a simple raise of the arms or fist pump after he scored a big goal. For example, when Logan scored the game-winning goal in overtime last year at the Provincial championships, all he did was raise his arms in the air before he got mauled by his teammates. Logan didn't see the need to make a big deal out of scoring a goal when he was only doing his job.

As the practice neared its end, Logan and the rest of the players wondered if it was time for the dreaded gauntlet.

"Alright, well this would be time for the gauntlet. But I'm sure you all heard about Scott's injury this morning, so we'll just skate you instead," said Coach Vixen. "That should be just as—if not more—painful than the gauntlet," the coach added with a fearsome smile on his face.

Some players breathed a collective sigh of the relief while others were devastated. Logan never enjoyed skating at the end of practices, but if he had to choose between a bag skate made of several repetitive, strenuous skating drills and sprints and going through the gauntlet with a nutcase like Luke Brown on the loose, he would choose the bag skate every single time.

Chapter 12

      The next morning, Logan turned on the television to watch Sportsnet Connected on Sportsnet Pacific before he made his way down to the arena with the guys. First, he saw some highlights from the Major League Baseball pennant races which were well on their way. Logan had never been much of a baseball fan; however, he always used to pay attention down the stretch and into the playoffs. Next was a feature on Matt Orr, a defence-man of the Vancouver Canucks who had recently been involved in many trade talks around the league. Lastly, as Logan looked for the remote to switch off the television, he noticed that Sportsnet Connected was running a feature updating the viewers on the first day of the Canucks prospect tryout. Logan saw some footage of the first group doing the gauntlet yesterday, and they caught Scott Bell's injury and him leaving the ice favouring his right shoulder on camera. Logan had no idea the media had come to the tryout yesterday, but it soon became evident that the media and fans would pay close attention to anything regarding their beloved Vancouver Canucks. Luckily, Logan didn't have a run in with Luke Brown as he descended in the elevator this time around. Today it came shortly after.

"Nice move you made on Jackson there yesterday, Watter," said Luke Brown as the players made their way to the bus parked out front of the hotel.

Logan was certain that Luke hadn't transformed into a totally different person overnight, so he was just waiting for a degrading comment to come out of his mouth.

"Thanks," Logan said.

"Yeah, try that on me today, and I'll put you flat on the ice, face first, kid," said Luke.

"I'll keep that in mind," Logan answered as he hopped into the bus, followed closely by Luke.

Logan had already become accustomed to Luke's constant razzing; while he obviously didn't particularly enjoy it, it didn't really bother him much anymore, either. When the bus arrived at General Motors Place, the players didn't need to be ushered to their respective destinations in the building. Group two, Logan and Luke's group, would head straight to the dressing rooms to start putting all of their equipment on, while group one, Scott Bell's group, would head directly to the training room to jump on the stationary bike.

"Anyone know what we're doing out there today, boys?" Frank Dempster asked as Logan and the rest of the group put on their gear in the dressing room.

"Why don't you ask Watter? I'm sure he was chatting up Coach Vixen last," yelled Luke Brown. A few of the players laughed while the others continued to mind their own business.

Logan was tempted to simply deny Luke's foolish accusations, but he decided to use the reverse psychology technique and go along with Luke's joke instead, because he knew that that would get him all riled up even more.

"We weren't talking about hockey," Logan said as everyone in the room except for Luke burst out into laughter.

I can't believe I just said that, Logan thought as he continued to tie up his skates.

Soon after, the chatter died down considerably as it became closer to the time to hit the ice. Just like the day before, the intensity and focus in the room increased significantly as the useless chitchat came to an end. Logan had finished putting on all his equipment except for his helmet about five minutes before everyone else, and since he didn't want to be the first one out, he decided to re-tighten his skates. He waited a few minutes and as some of the others started making their way to the ice, Logan strapped on his helmet and decided to do the same.

"Alright boys, you really don't have much time to make an impression. No one stood out too much yesterday, so you're all still at the same level in our books, but that could change soon. So let's make the most out of our opportunity here," Coach Vixen said passionately, addressing the group at the partition between the benches after their light warm-up skate. "That's it from me," he concluded.

"You know the drill, guys: Three hard laps backwards and forwards. Let's start with backwards today," said the Assistant Coach. "What are you waiting for?!" he yelled, and each and every one of the players rapidly jumped to their feet and started to skate around the rink as the Assistant Coach continued to spew out more hockey jargon.

By the tone of Coach Vixen's voice coupled with the Assistant Coach's short loss of temper, Logan knew the

Coaches, at least, had definitely picked up the intensity for day two of tryouts, and he was sure they expected the players to do the same. This time, Logan was in the middle of the pack skating backwards, but that didn't bother him since he'd never been a strong backwards skater. However, he leapfrogged the majority of the players as they made the switch to forwards skating, and he was among the leaders throughout the final three laps.

That's more like it, he thought as he made his way to the bench following the warm-up skate.

"Wow, trying to prove something out there, Logan?" asked Brent Jackson as he came up behind Logan at the players' bench.

"Actually, I am." Logan chuckled as he offered Brent the water bottle.

"Where did you get those legs?" Brent asked as he drenched himself in water.

"All I did was work on skating back home, man—I had to, with my size," Logan answered as Coach Vixen blew the whistle and the players crowded around him.

The first drill Coach Vixen decided to carry out was none other than the dreaded gauntlet. The gauntlet was usually held at hitting clinics in minor hockey to teach the players the correct way to throw a body check, or at the end of practices to punish the players rather than bag skating them, but never at the start of a practice like Logan and the rest of the prospects were about to go through. Logan wondered why the coaches decided to continue with the gauntlet drill after all, especially after Scott Bell's injury, which had turned out to be a separated shoulder.

"If you can't take a body check against your own friends and teammates in a practice, you won't be able to take one against your enemies in an actual game," said Coach Vixen as the players lined up one meter away from the boards.

Once all the players had lined up, the Coach slowly skated down the line, wondering which player he should choose to go through the gauntlet first. Logan held his breath as he saw Coach Vixen coming up behind him.

Not first, I can't be first, Logan thought to himself.

Logan breathed a sigh of relief when Coach Vixen skated past him without signalling to anyone.

"I guess it's only fair to choose a rookie," Coach Vixen said as Logan and the few other rookies on the team attempted to avoid eye contact with the Coach.

"Logan Watt, come on down; you're on The Price is Right," yelled Coach Vixen from the front of the line.

"Fantastic," Logan sarcastically muttered under his breath as he skated towards Coach Vixen.

"Fantastic," said Luke Brown eagerly and excitedly as he waited, first in line, to get a licking in on the rookie.

As Coach Vixen went over the rules of the drill, Logan wondered if he should skate as fast as he could down the boards and let his speed absorb the physical contact he was about to receive, or if he should skate slowly and brace himself as each player went at him. Logan decided he would go down the line full speed and hope to avoid as many body checks as possible. When Coach Vixen blew the start whistle, Logan didn't hesitate at all. He dug his recently sharpened skates into the ice and pushed off with brute strength, starting off so quickly that Luke Brown, who was first in line, made a complete fool out of himself attempting to hit Logan. Logan flew past him, and Luke ran into the boards. Logan avoided a few more checks along the way; however, he also got plastered into the boards on more than one occasion. It took Logan about a minute to go through all of the players along the line. He immediately knew he'd have to pull out the ice pack later tonight, but he was also thankful that he hadn't been seriously injured like Scott.

The rest of the gauntlet drill took about half of the practice before Coach Vixen decided to switch things up. He proceeded to give a speech about how important cycling and down-low play was in hockey in this day and age, so he wanted to see how the players could perform in the corners. "Alright, three on threes on down-low; make your own groups and we'll get started," he finished.

Logan paired up with Frank Dempster and Brent Jackson. Logan and Frank provided the speed while Brent provided the muscle. They were the first group up against Jack Patel, the only American in the group; Zach Campbell from the Ontario Hockey League; and, of course, Luke Brown.

"Battle for the puck in the corner for at least one minute before you try to bring it out and score a goal; first team that scores a goal after a minute wins, and the team that loses has to do a set of lines," Coach Vixen said as Logan and Luke's groups prepared to get started.

Coach Vixen dumped the puck into the corner from center, blew his whistle, and all six players entered the zone with the goal of fishing the puck out of the corner and cycling it down low. Logan was the first to the puck, but he saw Luke coming at him with full force, so he passed it behind the net, where Frank Dempster was waiting diligently. Frank saw Brent Jackson wide open at the point, but they needed to have possession of the puck for a minute before they were allowed to go for a goal, so he passed it back to Logan in the corner. Logan skated up along the boards and then noticed that Brent Jackson had curled around the net and was coming up behind him along the boards, so Logan dropped the puck back from his backhand right onto Brent's stick. Brent saw that Frank Dempster had curled around the net as well, so he proceeded to drop the puck back to Frank along the boards. Frank did the same until Logan finally received the puck along the boards for a second time. They were executing the cycle to perfection.

"Alright, one minute is up. Go for goal," yelled Coach Vixen as Logan had the puck on the half boards with a little bit of space to work with.

Logan went in right at Luke Brown and faked a slap shot; he then made his way into the middle of the ice and released a quick yet powerful wrist shot. The goaltender kicked out his right pad and saved Logan's shot; however, he let out a juicy rebound in the process, and Frank Dempster tapped it in as he crashed into the net hard with Jack Patel hounding him from behind.

"Atta boy, Dempster," Logan said as he went over to congratulate Frank on the goal.

"Thanks, nice shot there, eh," Frank answered as he, Logan, and Brent skated over to the benches to get some water.

"Jack, Zach, Luke, one set of lines now!" yelled Coach Vixen as the three of them, already gasping for air, made their way to the goal line.

That was the final drill of the day. Logan was rather satisfied with his performance; he hadn't scored a goal, but he felt like he was starting to get his legs back, and he'd performed well in the gauntlet and three-on-three drills.

The dry-land training following the on-ice session was no different than the day before except that Logan was really sore from the gauntlet and pretty tired from the whole practice in general. He wasn't looking forward to the ten-minute ride on the stationary bike which would undoubtedly add to the fatigue factor, but much to his surprise, he couldn't wait to start the yoga and get into that relaxation pose that he had already grown to love.

Chapter 13

As Logan had breakfast with the whole team at the Fairmont Hotel's restaurant the next morning, he thought about how much he was looking forward to finally getting into some game action. Coach Vixen had informed the group at last night's team meeting that today they would be having an intra-squad game. They would split the entire group up into two teams, and they would play against each other as if it were an actual game. Logan was excited, seeing as he was always better in game situations than in practice; but he was also somewhat worried because he had never really played with any of the guys before, and Coach Vixen hadn't gone over any systems, so it would basically be a free for all.

"You better hope you're on my team today, Watter," said Luke Brown as he followed Logan back up to the buffet for seconds.

"Yeah, and why is that?" asked Logan as he grabbed a croissant and a bagel from the pastry bin. "I would think you would want to be on *my* team so I don't make a complete fool out of you like I did yesterday," he added before he had a chance to think.

"You think you're tough, Watter? You haven't seen nothing yet, kid. Today you'll see what it's really like playing against men," Luke retorted as he picked Logan's bagel off his plate, took a bite out of it, and threw it back down.

Where have I heard that before? Logan thought as he threw the half-eaten bagel into the garbage and grabbed a fresh one from the bin.

When all the players arrived at General Motors Place, the team list for the intra-squad game was listed on the door of Coach Vixen's office. Logan waited for the initial crowd of players around the door to disintegrate before he checked out which team he was on. He was delighted to see he was on Team White with Brent Jackson, whom Logan had developed a nice little friendship with. Before he went off to the dressing room to get changed, Logan decided to check out which team Luke Brown was on. Logan put his finger on Luke's name and then dragged it in a straight line across the paper to read "Blue." Logan didn't know what to think. He was happy he wasn't on Luke's team, but he was also somewhat nervous that he'd have to go up against him, especially with all the threats he'd received.

"Logan, what team are you on?" asked Frank Dempster as he walked by the coach's office.

"Team White, how about you?" replied Logan as he picked up his hockey bag and started walking towards the players dressing room.

"Blue," said Frank. "Should be a dandy though, first game I've played since last spring," he added.

"Yeah, same deal for me...Well, this is my dressing room; good luck, man," said Logan as he opened up the dressing room door.

"Alright, you too, see you out there," replied Frank as he walked down the hall to Team Blue's dressing room.

The Hockey Farmer

There wasn't nearly as much chatter in the dressing rooms as the previous few days. Coach Vixen said to treat this intra-squad game like an actual regular season game, so that's what the guys were doing. Whenever someone had something to say, it was about hockey, it was about the game, and nothing else. Sean Townsend, the Assistant General Manager of the Vancouver Canucks who'd called Logan a few days ago, came down and made a speech in each of the dressing rooms. Logan hadn't talked to Sean since that one phone call, and he had actually never met the guy, but he recognized him right away from the fierce tone in his voice. Sean pretty much echoed the sentiments of Coach Vixen.

"This will be the one and only chance for a lot of you here today," he said. "Make the most of it, go one hundred and ten percent, because if you don't, you will regret it for the rest of your life—and I know that first hand," added Sean.

"It's like we're in the Stanley Cup Finals here, eh, Logan?" Brent Jackson whispered as Sean Townsend left the room.

"I guess that's how they want us to feel," Logan answered as he took a sip of Gatorade and continued putting his equipment on.

Coach Vixen came into each dressing room about five minutes before game time, going over what forward lines and defensive pairings he would like to see starting the game. He also stressed the importance of making the simple play rather than doing something out of the ordinary, because that's what the scouts and management would be looking for. They didn't want to see anything crazy that wouldn't work against seasoned veterans who have played in the National Hockey League for twenty years.

Before he knew it, Logan was at center ice, lining up on the right wing against Frank Dempster. He was starting the game as the first line right winger for Team White, and he wanted to start off with a bang. Logan's team won the face-off cleanly and immediately proceeded to make the simple play and dump the puck into the corner. The defence-man for Team Blue was first to the puck, followed closely by Logan's strong fore-check. The defence-man reversed the puck to his partner behind the net before Logan had a chance to get there, but right as he passed the puck, Logan stapled the defence-man into the boards with emphasis. Logan had never been the most physical player, but he definitely looked like one on that play. He was going out of his comfort level against the coaches' wishes, but it seemed to be working for him.

Midway through the first period, the game was still scoreless. There hadn't been many chances either; however, there was a lot of aggressiveness and physical play going on. Logan was worried about how they'd all adjust to playing with new teammates, and ten minutes into the period, the unfamiliarity was apparent. There was little, if any, flow to the game, and both teams were very sloppy, especially in the offensive zone. Most of the passes were not tape to tape, and it seemed like the majority of the shots taken—which wasn't a lot—missed the net by a mile. No one really stood out either; Coach Vixen needed something, someone to step up and make a play. Logan shared the same sentiments.

I've done nothing, and I'm still right in the thick of things, Logan thought to himself as he took a breather on the players' bench.

This is perfect; the coaches are looking for anything right now. I need to do something, I need to make a play, Logan went on as he felt a tap on the back of a shoulder from Coach Vixen, indicating that he would be going out next shift.

Brent Jackson took the puck behind his own net so the rest of the players on his team could make a change. Both teams decided to make full line changes. Logan hopped over the boards and made his way to the half boards on the far side, where he would wait for the pass from Brent Jackson.

"Logan, come take the puck, I need to change it up!" yelled Brent Jackson from behind the net.

Logan remembered when he'd seen Josh Irvin of the Calgary Flames pick up the puck behind the net, go end to end and score a spectacular goal a few years back against the Edmonton Oilers. With the other team in the middle of the line change, this would be the best time to attempt to duplicate Irvin's work of art.

Here goes nothing, thought Logan as he skated behind the net with speed to pick up the puck from Brent Jackson.

Once Logan had the puck on his stick, he took a quick look up the ice to see if he could make a stretch pass to any of his teammates, but most of the players from both teams were cluttered around the players' benches, so he decided to stick with the original plan and skate with the puck. Logan felt as though he'd lost the puck, so he looked down for a couple seconds to regain control. When Logan looked back up, he saw Luke Brown lining him up for a big body check. Logan decided he would act as if he didn't see Luke coming, and then make a move at the last second. It was a risky move, but Logan felt it was the right one. Logan looked right but kept an eye on Luke coming from the left with his peripheral vision. As Luke was about to initiate contact, Logan turned on an extra gear and sped directly past Luke, leaving him completely out of the play and way out of position. Logan continued on with the puck; he had gotten through his own zone and the neutral zone without a hitch, now only the offensive zone was left. Logan crossed the opposing blue line but realized he would have to pass two defence-men to make it to the net, and he wasn't too confident he could do that without losing the puck or getting thrown to the ice. He had two options: He could make a quick stop and turn towards the boards, delaying the offence until his teammates got into the play, or he could use his speed and skate around the net.

I have too much speed to stop now, Logan thought to himself as he quickly came to a decision.

Logan skated around the net at top flight with his head on a swivel, looking for a lane to shoot or to feed the puck to one of his teammates. By this time, Logan had already curled around the net and was now once again approaching the blue line; he would have to make a decision immediately, or else he would put all of his teammates offside. Logan noticed Zach Campbell was sneaking towards the net at the far side of the ice. Without giving it any further thought, Logan winded up and executed the back-door slap pass to perfection; Zach received the puck and one-timed it into the back of the net. Zach, along with everyone else in the building, was

The Hockey Farmer

surprised that Logan didn't shoot the puck. But with such flawless execution, it appeared they had practiced this play almost religiously. Team White had taken a 1-0 lead, and kept that lead going into the first intermission. Once again, without actually scoring a goal, Logan had made a positive impression on Coach Vixen and everyone else watching the game.

The second period was even more dull and uneventful than the first, if that was at all possible. At least the first had one goal thanks to Logan's end to end rush, but the second had nothing at all resembling a scoring opportunity. Unless you count Luke Brown's slap shot from the point, which would have looked like a routine if the goaltender hadn't given it the full roundabout when he caught it with his trapper. The physical play and strong defensive awareness from both teams carried on into the second—no one could question the passion or intensity in this intra-squad game, but just its entertainment value.

Logan started off the third period on the right wing as usual, but was surprised to see Luke Brown lining up against him, when Luke had played defence the whole game up until that point.

"Why the sudden switch in positions?" Logan asked Luke before the third period puck drop.

"You'll find out soon, little boy," Luke said as the referee dropped the puck and the third period got underway.

What is that supposed to mean? Logan wondered as he went back into his own zone to open up a lane for an outlet pass for his defence-man.

Logan received the pass, curled back behind his net and then made a long stretch pass to center ice, where Zach

Campbell was waiting. The play quickly progressed as Zach entered the attacking zone with the puck. One of the defence-men on Logan's team pinched up into the play so Logan held back to cover for him. For some odd reason, so did Luke Brown. While all eyes in the building were on Zach Campbell dangling in the offensive zone, Luke decided to make his move on Logan behind the play.

"Alright, let's just settle this once and for all and drop the gloves, kid," said Luke as Logan approached the neutral zone.

"I have nothing to settle with you," said Logan, not at all interested in what Luke had to say.

"So are you saying you don't want to fight me?" asked Luke.

"That's pretty much what I'm saying," said Logan, not overly excited to drop the gloves with a player that basically made fighting a way of life.

"Wrong answer," said Luke as he wound up and viciously slashed Logan's left wrist. "Welcome to Vancouver, Watter," Luke added as Logan immediately dropped to the ice, and Luke quickly re-entered the play before anyone on the ice noticed that Logan was injured.

Chapter 14

"Well, it doesn't look too serious, but you definitely won't want to risk making it any worse," said John Stevenson, the team's doctor, as Logan sat in the dressing room, wishing he was on the ice finishing the game.

"So when do you think is the earliest time I'll be able to play again?" asked Logan. "What is the best case scenario?"

"Well, Logan, the best case scenario is that your wrist will be fully healed in two weeks," said the doctor.

Two weeks is too long. I need to be back before the end of the week so I can show the coaches I'm not just a little fragile teenager, Logan thought.

"But can't I play before it's fully healed? Because I really need to be back on the ice before the end of the week," Logan added.

"Well, son, we still have to run a few more tests, but unless I find something completely out of the ordinary, the absolute earliest you'll be able to play again is in ten days," said the doctor as he saw Logan's face turn from hope to dejection. "I'll talk to Coach Vixen and let him know about the situation. I wouldn't worry about it; I'm sure he'll understand," the doctor added, trying to raise Logan's spirits.

Logan wasn't so sure. He immediately wondered if this wrist injury was a sign; he wondered if he was destined never to become a professional hockey player after all. The only thing that had kept Logan from being drafted this past summer was his size and the question of whether or not he could handle the physical aspect of the National Hockey League. With this injury, Logan doubted he would be given another opportunity to prove that he could handle the aggression that came hand in hand with playing at the next level.

Maybe if I told them what actually happened, they would give me another chance? Logan wondered as he sat in the dressing room all alone, pondering his situation. *But I don't want to be known as someone who rats people out or makes excuses for his poor performance or injuries. I'm not gonna make a fool out of myself by accusing one of the veteran players of basically attacking me, even if that's exactly what Luke did.*

Logan then thought about what his father had taught him growing up and on the farm this summer: If you run into a problem, don't run away from it, just deal with it head on. In these first few days at Canucks prospects camp, Logan had gotten a taste of what it was like to be a National Hockey League player, and he definitely enjoyed the feeling. He wasn't about to give up his dreams and goals now just because one goof had made it his goal to injure Logan. He had run into a major speed bump, but now all he had to do was work harder to achieve his ambitions. And if the Vancouver Canucks didn't give him another shot, he would work even harder and find somewhere else to play. He wasn't about to throw in the towel.

The Hockey Farmer

Logan's plane ticket wasn't scheduled until the end of the week, so he would have to watch his friends and enemies battle for a spot with the Canucks as he put on a fake smile and cheered from the sidelines. Logan would have liked to head back to Cochrane and help his father finish up the work on the farm while doing everything he could to rehab his wrist. However, if he asked for an earlier flight out of town, he wouldn't seem like a team player. So Logan decided he would stick it out, say all the right things and do all the right things during the rest of his stay in the big city. But little did he know that his ability to say all of the right things would be put to the test after the intra-squad game as the Vancouver sports media chose Logan as their flavour of the week.

"What happened to your wrist?"
"Are you out for the season?"
"What's the diagnosis?"
"Did someone attack you?"

Logan took a minute to think about what he was going to say as a dozen of reporters crowded around him and waved a wide variety of tape recorders and microphones in his face. To say that Logan was overwhelmed would have been a complete and massive understatement. As a child, Logan used to practice answering these types of questions with politically correct hockey answers. But this time, rather than talking to himself in the mirror, he was talking to professional sports journalists and reporters. This was the real deal.

"Well, I don't know what the official diagnosis is— you would have to ask the doctor for that. All I know is that he told me I'll be out for at least ten days," said Logan.

"How disappointed are you, and have you talked to Coach Vixen about your future with the Canucks?" asked a reporter from Team 1040, the local sports radio station in Vancouver.

"Well, I'm obviously very disappointed. The Canucks gave me a prime opportunity to showcase my stuff, and with this injury, I won't be able to do that to the fullest extent. It's definitely a tough break, but now I'm just going to have to work harder to get where I want to eventually get. As for my future with the team, I haven't had the chance to speak with Coach Vixen yet, so your guess is as good as mine," said Logan, sounding like he'd dealt with the media his whole life.

"What actually happened out there?" yelled a reporter from the back of the media scrum.

Logan took another moment before he answered.

"Well, I took a hit from Luke Brown, and I guess my wrist ended up in an awkward position. I guess it's impossible to prevent these types of freak injuries," Logan said, feeling a hint of shame for lying to the reporters.

"Luke usually picks a rookie to torment each year; is it safe to say you're that guy this year?" asked a reporter from Sportsnet Pacific.

"Well, I'm not sure, because I don't really pay attention to which rookies he torments. However, I can tell you that Luke's role is to be an agitator, and he is very good at what he does. If he wasn't getting on my nerves and on those of every other player in this dressing room, he wouldn't be doing his job," responded Logan, with the politically correct answer.

At that point, Logan hoped the scrum of reporters would move on, but that was not the case—the questions just kept on coming.

"Are you going back to Cochrane now that you're out for the duration of the tryout?"

"Actually, my flight isn't until the weekend, so I'll be sticking around with the team until the tryout is over."

"What are your plans if you get released by the Vancouver Canucks?"

"If that time comes, I'll take some time and think about what my best options are, and then I'll be sure to let you guys know. But as of now, I've heard nothing from Coach Vixen or any of the Vancouver Canucks management, and unless I do, I can't be worrying about that kind of stuff," responded Logan, hoping he wouldn't have to make that decision.

"But is it safe to say that you will continue playing hockey, even if it isn't at the professional or semi-professional level?"

"Like I said, I haven't thought about that yet, but if it comes to a point where I have to consider it, you guys will be the first to hear from me."

"So does that mean you're considering retiring from hockey if you don't make the team?"

"Next question," said Logan.

Logan began to realize why so many professional hockey players always came across as rude and obnoxious towards the media. They basically kept on asking the same questions over and over again, and Logan had to somehow change his answers for each of the questions. It was not an easy feat, and it could be very frustrating. Logan started to realize a large chunk of the reporters and journalists here in

Vancouver were ruthless when it comes to their business. They would say anything and ask any question, no matter what the relevance, to get the answers they thought would make a good story. They asked questions to essentially put words in the player's mouth.

Logan was surprised that none of the reporters seemed to have more questions. He waited a few moments, just to give them all one last opportunity to throw out some more useless and redundant questions, but they didn't take it. So, finally, Logan was able to end the interview on a good note.

"Thanks a lot, guys, see you tomorrow," Logan said as the other players entered the room and half the media assemblage immediately wallowed towards Luke Brown, and the other half left the room looking to have a chat with Coach Vixen.

I probably shouldn't have said that, Logan thought as he finally got an ounce of breathing room. *I basically invited them to come and bombard me with questions tomorrow just like they did today.*

As Logan sat in his stall waiting for Coach Vixen to address the group like he did after each practice, Logan noticed an attractive female who appeared to be around the same age as him, who had just entered the dressing room. She had a head of dark brown hair, beautiful bright sky blue eyes, and appeared to be more or less the same height as Logan. She was dressed in a modern and very stylish dark blue business suit with white pinstripes. Logan never knew a business suit could look so good on a woman; he was so impressed that he thought that her outfit could be pulled off as a casual outfit that would be worn to a party rather than a business suit to wear on the job. Logan wondered what a teenage girl of this nature would be doing in the Vancouver Canucks dressing room, so he decided to keep a close eye on her, for more than one reason. After all, Logan was a teenage boy. She opened up her briefcase-like bag and pulled out a digital voice recorder.

She couldn't be a reporter, could she? Logan wondered. *She must just look around my age; she's probably a lot older.*

Logan continued to watch her. She saw the big media scrum around Luke Brown so she went towards it but wasn't able to get close enough to get any sort of sound bite. She then took a quick look around the room and noticed Logan sitting in his stall alone with an ice pack on his wrist. Logan quickly looked away so he didn't appear to be staring at her, and then she started towards his stall.

"Hi there, I'm Samantha McMillan," said the woman, with a glowing smile on her face that could have lit up the whole room.

"Logan Watt," he answered.

All of a sudden, Logan felt a hint of nervousness go through his body. He had just been interviewed by a wolf pack of reporters and felt nothing. But now simply talking to one good-looking female reporter seemed to have a completely different effect on him.

Logan and Samantha locked eyes for a few moments without saying a word to each other. Samantha appeared to share the same feelings of anxiety as Logan and consequently was at a loss for words. Logan, on the other hand, had completely blocked out everything from his mind including the farm, his injury, Luke Brown, and his future in hockey and just simply stared at Samantha, mesmerized by her alluring and elegant smile.

Chapter 15

The absolute last things on Samantha's mind were hockey or work, but she wanted to do or say anything to end the awkward silence between her and Logan because it was fairly obvious that Logan wasn't going to say a word. And after all, she was here to get a sound bite from the players and coaches. "So, can I get a quick interview with you?" she asked.

"Uhh, yeah yeah, for sure, no problem," replied Logan, also relieved that the awkward silence had come to an end. "You wouldn't be the first one today."

"So I'm assuming you had to deal with the crazy media huddle over there?" said Samantha as she looked over to all the reporters swarming around Luke Brown's stall.

"Yeah, they actually just left my stall before you walked in," Logan said, unintentionally admitting he'd watched her as she entered the dressing room. "I think 'crazy' is definitely the right word to describe them," he added as he and Samantha shared a laugh for the first time.

"Oh, after a couple days talking to them, it will become second nature to you. But one thing you need to know is that if you make the team, they will follow your every move, and you will always be in the public

The Hockey Farmer

spotlight," Samantha said, pleased that she was actually having a nice, normal conversation with Logan.

"Well, that's a sacrifice I would definitely be willing to make if I made the big leagues," answered Logan, also pleased with the fluent conversation he was having with Samantha. "Besides, I'm a pretty boring guy anyways, so I don't think they would find anything too interesting about me," he added.

"I'm sure that's not true," said Samantha, becoming interested to learn more about Logan. "And believe me, they can make the biggest deal out of any little aspect of your life—and I would know, because I'm becoming one of them."

Logan chuckled.

"Alright, well, I better get that interview with you."

"Yeah let's do it."

The interview wasn't much different from the one Logan had with the other reporters just moments before Samantha had entered the room. She asked Logan about his wrist injury, how he thought he'd performed so far, if he has been notified by the Canucks organization regarding his future with the team, and what he needed to work on to ultimately make it to the next level. Logan was impressed by Samantha's articulation and knowledge for the Canucks and the game of hockey, while Samantha was impressed with Logan's politically correct hockey answers. Even though Samantha and Logan were talking about hockey, they both clearly had other things on their mind.

"So how long are you in town for?" asked Samantha, off the record, as she finished the interview and turned off the voice recorder.

"I'm here until the end of the week," said Logan. "Sucks that I'll have to watch instead of play, though."

"Yeah, I can only imagine," responded Samantha. "So I don't know if you've seen much of the city, but since I've lived here my whole life, I could show you around if you have time," said Samantha, hoping she hadn't completely freaked Logan out. "Only if you want," she added, since Logan didn't respond immediately.

"Well, we went to a few places on the first day like Science World, Granville Island, and the Capilano Suspension Bridge, but if you have anywhere else in mind, I would love to hang out," said Logan politely.

"I know a great ice cream place just across the street from Stanley Park," Samantha suggested.

"I like ice cream, and now that I'm out for the week, I don't exactly have to worry too much about my diet," responded Logan.

"Perfect," said Samantha.

"Perfect," echoed Logan as he saw Coach Vixen at the door waving at Logan, motioning for him to come into his office when he was done with the interview.

Samantha gave Logan her number, and then they parted ways. Samantha went towards Luke Brown's stall, where the crowd of reporters had significantly died down, while Logan, with his future in hockey back on his mind, nervously made his way out of the dressing room to Coach Vixen's office.

"Logan, come on in," said Coach Vixen as Logan entered his nice, spacious office. "Have a seat. How's the wrist feeling?"

"It's not too bad," said Logan.

The Hockey Farmer

"That's good to hear," said Coach Vixen. "So the doctor tells me you're done for at least ten days."

"Unfortunately, that's what he told me, too," responded Logan.

"Tough break, kid. So do you know what exactly happened to the wrist?"

"Umm, well, it was sort of in an awkward position when Luke hit me, so it must have got twisted or something," replied Logan, feeling as if he were back in the dressing room being interviewed for a second time as he explained his made up story about how he got hurt yet again.

"Well, that really is unfortunate because we thought you were having a really great game, and a really great tryout overall," said Coach Vixen.

"Thanks," said Logan, wondering if Coach Vixen was just saying that to raise his spirits before he was cut, or if he actually spoke the truth.

"But I talked to management and we all agree that with this injury, we won't be able to give you a spot on this team at the current time," said Coach Vixen.

"I can't say I'm surprised," said Logan, clearly disappointed and dejected.

"Sorry, kid," said Coach Vixen.

"You're just doing your job."

"But I wouldn't stop trying, son," Coach Vixen went on. "I'll tell you again that you have skill, and we really liked what he saw from you. So we'll definitely be keeping you on our radar. Just keep working, Logan, and you will make it; I guarantee it," added the Coach.

"Will do," said Logan as he got up off the couch and left the room.

Logan was obviously saddened by the news he had just received from Coach Vixen, but at the same time, he was honoured with the coach's closing remarks. Coach Vixen had just basically guaranteed that if Logan continued to work hard, he would in fact eventually end up in the National Hockey League. At first, Logan had thought Coach Vixen was just complimenting his play so that he didn't feel as bad when he was released by the team, but after the Coach's closing remarks, he realized Coach Vixen was speaking from the bottom of his heart. He thought that Logan had the skills to play professional hockey, and Logan knew Coach Vixen was a pretty smart guy when it came to judging potential in hockey players. So he wasn't about to go against the Coach's advice. He would keep trying; he would keep working hard, and he wouldn't take no for an answer.

Since the team had another function to attend later that evening, Logan decided he would give Samantha a call tomorrow after the team's practice. Even though Logan wasn't going to be on the ice, he was still expected to be around the team and in the arena. After Logan's meeting with Coach Vixen, he, along with the rest of the team, headed back to the hotel to get some rest before the team function. Logan was happy that the function was going to take place at the Fairmont Hotel's Ballroom so he wouldn't have to leave the building. All that he and the rest of the team knew was that a guest speaker would join the group at the restaurant.

"Logan Watt, first class liar, who would have thunk it?" said Luke Brown as he stood next to Logan in the elevator at the Fairmont Hotel.

The Hockey Farmer

"Are you complaining?" asked Logan, hoping the elevator would go faster so he could get back into his room and jump into his bed.

"Not at all, Watter," responded Luke. "But just for the record, I don't need you protecting me, and by not telling everyone what really happened, you're not scoring any points with me."

"Fine by me," said Logan.

"Good," said Luke. "How's the wrist feeling, by the way?" he asked sarcastically.

"Great, thanks," responded Logan.

"Well, here we are. It was nice knowing you, Watter, good luck back in Alberta. Maybe in your next lifetime," said Luke as he laughed and exited the elevator. "See ya, wouldn't wanna be ya!" he yelled as he made his way down the hallway.

Logan hadn't expected Luke to thank him for not ratting him out to the coach and media, but he had at least expected some hospitality for the good deed. But that had just been wishful thinking—kindness and appreciation certainly weren't in Luke Brown's nature.

Who was I kidding? This guy wouldn't save a helpless little child if it didn't somehow benefit him, and he would probably push the kid in front of a train if he thought he could get something out of it, Logan thought as he exited the elevator and pulled out the key card from his back pocket to open the door of his room.

Logan had already showered at the arena, so he immediately jumped into bed once he got back to his room. He picked up the remote and switched on the television, hoping to see some more coverage on the Vancouver Canucks. Even though Vancouver was a hockey-crazed city that paid attention to every little move regarding the Canucks, they couldn't have 24-hour coverage of the team. Logan was hoping to see his name on the television, even if it was saying that he was cut by the team, but instead, the International Tour of Poker, live from Japan, was on Sportsnet Pacific.

"Ughh," Logan moaned. *Who watches people play cards?* he wondered as he flickered through the channels.

Logan turned to channel 24, where he noticed Much Music was in the process of showing a marathon of *The OC* episodes. If anything was going to get his mind off hockey, his injury, and the disappointment of getting cut by the Vancouver Canucks for at least a few hours, it was a teenage action-packed series full of a whole lot of fighting, women, and drama. Logan put the remote back on his bedside table, kicked back a few iced teas, got his wrist into a comfortable position, and vegged out watching the life of a group of teenagers growing up in Orange County.

Chapter 16

"And with that, I would like to present to you our guest speaker for the evening, the one and the only... Todd Lang," said Coach Vixen at the team's banquet-like dinner at the Fairmont Hotel's in-house restaurant. Everyone in attendance put their hands together for the legend of the city of Vancouver.

Logan was a huge Todd Lang fan. Before being offered a tryout with the Vancouver Canucks, Lang had been the only Canucks player Logan actually liked and enjoyed watching. Partly because he too was born and raised in Alberta, in Camrose to be exact, and partly because Lang was one of the most respected and honourable players in the entire National Hockey League. Lang was the true definition of a gentleman on and off the ice. He was always a great leader in the dressing room vocally, and he always led by example with his work ethic and positive attitude on the ice. Logan had always tried to model himself around Todd Lang—not so much as a player, because they played with completely different styles, but as a person and as a leader. Logan couldn't wait to hear what he would have to say to the group, and he hoped he would get the privilege to have a one-on-one chat with Lang, one of the current Vancouver Canucks Assistant Captains, following his address.

"Looking at all of you here today reminds me of when I was your age, listening to Steven Schultz, who was my idol at the time, talking to us at the Canucks prospects camp—which, despite my receding hair line, wasn't too long ago," said Todd Lang as almost everyone in the Ballroom laughed quietly. "This goes to show that every single one of you has the opportunity to make the National Hockey League and make a name for yourself. I was like a lot of you: A skinny little kid who no one thought had a chance in the big leagues, and at times I doubted myself too, to the point where I almost decided to stop playing hockey permanently." Right away, Logan thought about how he had all but given up on playing hockey professionally this summer.

"But here I am. I'd like to think I've done alright and proven some critics wrong. I talked to Coach Vixen, and he's confident that this is one of the best groups we've had in a while, and a lot of you have a good chance to do something with your hockey careers," said Lang.

Lang went on for a few more minutes, talking about what it was like being a professional hockey player and all the hurdles he'd had to overcome to get where he was today. The theme of his speech was to work hard, have a positive attitude, and stay respectful, and with that everything would work out the way it was supposed to. He talked about how, at times, the life of a professional hockey player can be very overwhelming and stressful, and as a result he emphasized that every single player should have something to go back to that would keep their mind off hockey for a little while. That way, they could always come back to the rink with smiles on their faces and always enjoying what they do. For Lang, his diversion was cycling,

The Hockey Farmer

which was another thing he and Logan had in common. But along with the cycling, for Logan, going back home to work on the farm did the trick. This summer, Logan had learned that he didn't particularly enjoy farming on a daily basis, but that didn't mean he wouldn't love to go back every once in a while just to get his mind off of everything else.

As Todd finished up his speech and retook his seat next to Coach Vixen, Sean Townsend, and the rest of the Vancouver Canucks staff and management in attendance, Logan peered over to Luke Brown to see if he had taken Todd's words to heart. While Logan wasn't about to tell the coaches how he'd actually gotten injured, Logan had a slight glimpse of hope that with Todd's words, Luke would take a stand and admit to brutally slashing Logan's wrist for no apparent reason. However, Todd's address appeared to have no effect whatsoever on Luke Brown's character.

"Heart warming speech there, eh, Watter?" said Luke as he passed Logan's table. "Almost brought a tear to my eye," he added with a sarcastic tone that a two-year old could have easily detected.

Before Logan could say anything in return, Luke burst into laughter and made his way to the back of the room towards the buffet.

"You know you have some major issues when you crack up over your own jokes," said Brent Jackson, who was across from Logan at the same table.

Logan laughed out loud. "And here I actually thought Todd's speech might actually have some sort of positive effect on him," he said as he wiped his plate clean of fries.

"Well, if you thought that, you may be dumber than him," said Brent as he and Logan tried to contain their laughter when they saw Luke pass by their table again with another plate full of food.

Logan spent the most of the evening staring over at Todd's table, closely examining his every move. Logan had never actually met a National Hockey League player, so he was just itching at the opportunity to have a conversation with Todd. But on the other hand, he didn't want to seem like some immature little hockey fan looking for an autograph. So Logan attempted to observe Todd as discretely as he could while at the same time thinking about what he would say if he did actually end up talking to him.

"Just go talk to him, man," said Brent Jackson as he noticed Logan's fixation on the head table.

Logan quickly looked away from Todd. "Is it really that obvious?" he asked.

"You've been staring at him for the past twenty minutes; it's pretty obvious, man," replied Brent. "Believe me, you'll regret it if you don't," he added as he sipped the rest of the root beer from his tall glass.

"I don't want it to seem like I'm imposing, though," said Logan as he glanced back to Todd's table and noticed Todd was no longer there.

"So Coach Vixen tells me you grew up in Cochrane," said Todd Lang, who was suddenly standing right next to Logan's table.

Brent looked over at Logan with a big smile on his face.

"Uhh, yeah, I was actually born there and have lived there for my whole life," Logan responded, feeling

The Hockey Farmer

the same edginess he had when he was talking to Samantha after the intra-squad game.

"Oh really? That's pretty cool," said Todd as he pulled over a seat from the next table and took a sat adjacent to Logan. "I remember I actually played a few tournaments there back when I played minor hockey in Camrose—it's really a nice little city," he added pleasantly.

"Yeah, I like it, but I guess I haven't really seen much else," said Logan.

"That's true, but I'm sure that will soon change," Todd answered, as Logan wondered what he was trying to imply.

"I wouldn't mind calling Vancouver home," said Logan cheerfully.

"Well, keep doing what you're doing and from what I've heard, that could be a real possibility for you." Logan wondered if Todd was echoing the sentiments of Coach Vixen and the Canucks management or if it was just his personal opinion. "I better get going though. Just wanted to have a word with you and wish you good luck in the future. Hopefully we'll be playing together soon," added Todd.

"Thanks so much—it was nice meeting you," said Logan as he shook Todd's hand firmly.

"Take care, Logan." Todd walked back towards the head table and engaged in a short conversation with Coach Vixen before he left the restaurant.

Logan wondered why Todd had chosen to talk to him out of everyone in the room, but he wasn't complaining. *It couldn't be just because I'm from Alberta, too*, he thought.

"Hey, Watt, you're never going to wash your hand again, are you?" Brent said. He'd returned from the bathroom to see Logan shaking Todd's hand.

"Shut it, Jackson."

Chapter 17

The next day was simply another day of practicing at General Motors Place for the Canucks prospects. Logan came to the arena on the bus with the rest of the boys as usual, but once he got there, he didn't know what Coach Vixen expected him to do. He obviously couldn't take part in the on-ice session due to his wrist injury, and the doctor had advised him not to ride the stationary bike because it could aggravate the injury, so he couldn't take part in the dry-land training either. He couldn't even participate in the yoga session, as many of the poses called for pressure from leaning on the wrists. Logan decided that he would go straight to Coach Vixen's office once he arrived at General Motors Place to figure out what he could do while the others were either on the ice or in the training room.

"Logan, come on in," said Coach Vixen when Logan knocked on his office door.

"I was just wondering what I could do while the others are on the ice. The doctor said I can't take part in the fitness training or yoga session either." Logan took a seat on the sofa in Coach Vixen's office.

"Well, let's see here. Your left wrist is injured, right?" asked Coach Vixen.

"Yeah."

"And you write with your right hand, I'm assuming?"

"Yeah."

"Perfect, let me give you this list," said Coach Vixen as he opened up the drawer in his desk and started scrambling around some papers. "Ah, here it is."

"What is it, Coach?" asked Logan as Coach Vixen handed him the paper along with a pencil.

"It's a list of all the players in camp this year; you're going to head up to the press box and watch both practices so you can take some notes for me," said Coach Vixen in high spirits.

"Okay, sounds good, Coach, but what kind of stuff do you want me to look for?"

"Well, the boys don't know this yet, but we're going to have a little twenty-minute scrimmage at the end of each on-ice session today, so just note down stuff like shots on net, missed shots, blocked shots, and turnovers," responded Coach Vixen.

"That I can do," said Logan, disappointed that he would be missing out on another scrimmage and another shot to showcase his skills.

"I better get out on the ice; do you know how to get to the press box?" asked Coach Vixen as he got up off his chair and started towards the ice surface.

"I'll figure it out." Logan too got up and followed closely behind Coach Vixen as he exited the office.

Logan was right; he did figure it out, but only after a comprehensive adventure around General Motors Place. He'd never known that only one press box was open or that the upper level had so many different suites and rooms on it. Logan took the elevator to the upper level of the arena and walked around, attempting to open each and every door before he finally found the right one. Logan took a seat on the sofa and looked down on the Vancouver Canucks orca logo at center ice as players started trickling out of the dressing room and onto the ice.

The two hours up in the press box seemed like an eternity for Logan. He was at least thankful he had the notes for Coach Vixen to pay attention to, or else he was sure he would have passed out after the first on-ice session. However, Logan's full attention wasn't on shots on net, missed shots, blocked shots and turnovers; he couldn't help but look forward to the little date he had planned with Samantha after the two hours were up. He'd felt a connection with her the previous day in the dressing room, as they were both "rookies" so to speak, in unfamiliar waters. Logan was excited to find out whether that connection was real, or if it was just a figment of his imagination.

Logan found his way back down to the dressing room much more easily than his expedition to the press box. He went to the dressing room to talk to some of the guys as they took off all their equipment and then made his way back to Coach Vixen's office to give him all the stats that he had noted down from up above. Coach Vixen informed Logan that he and the rest of the players had the remainder of the day off, so they could hang around at the hotel or go off on their own around the city. Logan had already anticipated this, and had already made plans to meet up with Samantha at Stanley Park.

Once the bus dropped the group back to the hotel, Logan went up to his room to change his clothes. He didn't want to wear sweatpants and a hoodie on his first actual date with Samantha—if you could even call a simple walk around Stanley Park a "date." Logan put on some jean shorts and a white polo shirt. He took off his hat and went into the bathroom to gel his hair before he grabbed his sunglasses and left the room.

"Watt, where you headed, buddy?" asked Brent Jackson as he saw Logan come out of the elevator in the lobby.

Logan wasn't really too keen on letting anyone know he was going to meet a girl.

"Uhh, just going down to Stanley Park to meet an old friend," answered Logan, hoping Brent wouldn't question his response.

"Oh alright, cool. Well when you get back, come up to Frank's room—we're gonna hook up his Xbox 360 and play some Guitar Hero," said Brent as he pressed the up button on the elevator.

"Oh nice, I'll try to be back as soon as possible so I can own you all." Logan and Brent laughed, then took their separate ways.

Logan's walk to Stanley Park was short and uneventful. However, he passed a wide variety of people on his way. He saw people in business suits, in shorts and t-shirts, and even saw a few homeless people on the corners begging for money. Logan started to realize that Vancouver was a city of many different classes and cultures. The park was only a few blocks from the hotel, so Logan was there in about five minutes. Once he arrived, Logan didn't spot Samantha, so he pulled out his cell phone and gave her a call.

"Hey, Samantha, it's Logan."

The Hockey Farmer

"Oh hey, Logan, I just got to the park; I'm actually coming out of my car right now." Logan looked towards the parking lot and spotted Samantha. "Where are you?" she added as she started walking towards the park.

"You know what, I think I see you. Talk to you in a second," Logan said as he quickly hung up his phone, trying to protect his father from having a heart attack when he saw the long-distance call on the phone bill.

Logan and Samantha were both relieved when their conversation proved less awkward and nerve-wracking this time around than it had in the dressing room. When they talked, it seemed like they had been friends for years, and that connection seemed to bring the two of them closer together emotionally. The initial uneasiness between them was now in the past, and this time they were simply able to put all else aside and have a nice little walk around Stanley Park sharing a cotton-candy-flavoured ice cream cone.

"So how in the world did you land a job working for the Vancouver Canucks?" Logan asked Samantha as they walked down the path next to the ocean.

"Well, I'm actually in the communications program over at Simon Fraser University, and this summer I had the option to take some classes or do Co-op, which is a program where you get to apply for jobs in the field you're studying," answered Samantha. Logan was still impressed with how fluently and smoothly the words came out of her mouth.

"And I'm guessing you chose to take the Co-op route and applied for a job with the Canucks."

"Actually, both the Canucks and Lions. Hey, you're pretty smart for a hockey player," responded Samantha sarcastically.

"Oh, what is that supposed to mean—are all hockey players completely stupid?" Logan retorted as he playfully bumped shoulders with Samantha.

"You said it, not me," responded Samantha good-humouredly as she playfully bumped Logan back.

"Oh, so that's how it's gonna be then, is it?" Logan threw his ice cream cone in the garbage.

"I guess so," Samantha said with an innocent smile on her face.

Logan smiled back, and then the first awkward silence of the day was interrupted by Samantha's Avril Lavigne ring-tone.

"Ughh, I'm so sorry; I should probably answer this," said Samantha as she pulled her cell phone out of her purse.

"Yeah, yeah, of course," said Logan politely.

After a short conversation with her mother, Samantha slammed her phone shut and looked towards Logan embarrassingly.

"I'm so sorry, Logan. I have to go drop my little sister off at dance practice." Samantha was noticeably disappointed.

"No, no, don't worry about it, I should probably get back to the hotel, too," responded Logan, doing a much better job of concealing his disappointment.

"Maybe we could continue this conversation tomorrow over another cone of ice cream?" asked Samantha with a beautiful smile that Logan couldn't resist.

"Sounds good to me," he said cheerfully.

Samantha came towards Logan with her arms up in the air, looking for a good-bye hug. Logan put his hands around Samantha's waist as she leaned her head on his shoulders. Logan embraced her gently and, as they both pulled away, his hands tenderly grazed Samantha's lower back, accidentally-on-purpose. Samantha started walking to her car, and Logan wondered whether he had offended her with his short loss of control. Samantha turned around and showcased her sparkling smile one last time in Logan's direction, and he got his answer.

Logan watched Samantha drive away in her black Honda Civic, turned the other away and looked at the beautiful and peaceful Pacific Ocean. Then he went back towards the hotel to join the others on the Xbox 360.

Now this is the life, he thought.

Chapter 18

Logan hadn't slept much the previous night. He didn't have any life-altering decisions to make like earlier in the summer, but his time with Samantha made him ponder many thoughts as he attempted to get some rest. Logan was starting to become accustomed to the big city life, and much to his amazement, he was starting to like it. Growing up in a fairly small town in the outskirts of Calgary, which wasn't anywhere near the magnitude of Vancouver, Logan had never seen himself enjoying a big city like he was. Logan would admittedly always be a good old farmer from Cochrane, Alberta at heart, but he was starting to figure out that he wouldn't mind a life in Vancouver, British Columbia either.

Logan went down to the breakfast buffet at the Fairmont Hotel restaurant at around seven-thirty in the morning. Once he arrived downstairs, most of the players were already sitting down and enjoying their full-course meal consisting of scrambled eggs, hash browns, and toast. Logan considered going for the appealing meal but thought better of it and decided to stick to his traditional bagels and cream cheese.

Ugh, I could be upstairs in bed sleeping right now, Logan thought as he spread the cream cheese across both of his bagels.

The Hockey Farmer

Logan took a seat next to Frank Dempster and Brent Jackson at the table nearest the Coaches'. Logan was relieved that neither Brent nor Frank were in the mood to engage in any sort of conversation because, quite frankly, Logan just wanted to sit down and enjoy his bagels. Luckily for him, both of his teammates shared the same sentiment about their scrambled eggs, hash browns, and toast. Not much was said during their short time at the breakfast table, and that was a common theme for the other players around the restaurant as well. Logan had heard that since Coach Vixen gave the group the entire evening and night off, Luke Brown took a few of the other players out to a big house party in West Vancouver. Logan also heard that West Vancouver was the richest area in the entire lower mainland, and most houses in that vicinity cost no less than 1.5 million dollars. In addition, Frank told Logan that kids in West Vancouver had to pay almost triple the normal price to play minor hockey. Logan peered over to Luke Brown's table, and he was certainly no expert, but Luke appeared to be in the process of nursing a first-class hangover.

"Luke must have gotten trashed last night," said Logan as Brent and Frank looked over towards his table.

"Definitely looks like it. I can't see him going to a house party and not getting hammered, even if it costs him a spot on this team," said Frank as he turned away from Luke's table and refocused his attention on the remainders of his scrambled eggs severely covered in ketchup.

"He does it every year. I made the mistake of going with him last year—definitely wasn't a good idea," recalled Brent as he picked up his mug and sipped Irish coffee.

"Don't the coaches ever find out?" asked Logan quietly as he made a quick glance towards the Coaches' table to make sure they weren't listening in.

"Oh, I'm pretty sure they know all about what he does," answered Brent.

"Then why in the hell do they keep him around?" asked Frank as he wiped his plate clean of eggs.

"Well, my theory is that they keep him in the fold just to intimidate all of us other players," said Brent as Logan and Frank listened attentively. "They know he's a force on and off the ice, and they know that if we can't stand up to him, we're not going to be able to stand up to people in the big leagues who cause twice as much trouble as he does," added Brent as Logan noticed he had obviously given the subject some major thought.

"You think they know he two-handed me on the wrist and that's how I actually got hurt?" asked Logan hopefully

"They have people watching all over the building. I'm sure they know," said Brent as Logan recalled all the suspect people he'd noticed watching the practice when he was making his way up to the press box the other day.

Logan hoped that Brent was right and the coaching staff and team management knew all about how Logan was actually hurt. If they knew the truth, they would also know that Logan had had no opportunity to defend himself and prevent the unfortunate injury.

As Logan continued to watch Luke for no apparent reason, he noticed that Luke was drinking an excessive amount of orange juice and water, and even though Logan didn't drink, he knew orange juice and water were two of the greatest remedies for a hangover.

The Hockey Farmer

Who does this guy think he is? Logan thought as Coach Vixen got up and announced that the bus would be leaving in about ten minutes.

Logan really wasn't in the mood to sit in the press box and take notes again, but that was what he ended up doing. He was no use to the coaches otherwise, so he decided to act in accordance to their wishes with no questions asked. Logan wasn't about to become the teacher's pet, so to speak, but he wasn't going to do anything that would jeopardize his relationship with the coaching staff and possibly lay his chances for a second shot on the line.

When the group arrived at the arena, Logan had yet another slight encounter with Luke Brown. Luke was sticking to his intimidating and hostile nature, even if he had already knocked Logan out of the line-up for the duration of the tryouts.

"Watter, what's it like sitting up in the press box every day writing down how good I am?" Luke said as Logan waited for Coach Vixen to give him another team list.

"Luke, no one likes you," answered Logan. He felt no reason to hold back on insulting Luke now that the damage had already been done

"Shut up, Watter, or else I'll take out your other wrist, too," responded Luke furiously.

"Oh, I'm just shaking in my boots," Logan said, basically disregarding Luke's threats even though he was pretty sure they were not empty ones.

Before Luke had a chance to say or do anything to Logan, Coach Vixen walked by, and Luke's persona changed drastically.

"Playing nicely, boys?" said Coach Vixen as he took his keys out of his pocket and inserted them into the door.

"Of course," Luke answered immediately as Logan covered up his laughter with a phoney cough.

"Good, because if I found out you weren't, there would be some major consequences," Coach Vixen said in a calm and collected manner as he waved Logan into his office. "Luke, you should probably go get changed—you don't want to be late for practice like Jack was yesterday," added Coach Vixen, referring to all the skating Jack Patel had been forced to do because he was a mere thirty seconds late.

"On my way," Luke said. He stared at Logan, then picked up his bag and walked down the hallway into the team dressing room.

"What a fraud," said Coach Vixen under his breath as he took a seat at his desk and shuffled through some more papers to find the team list for Logan.

Coach Vixen's comments about Luke only confirmed to Logan that Brent Jackson's suspicions about how much the staff really knew were correct. Logan breathed a huge sigh of relief, as this recent turn of events essentially meant they knew exactly how Logan was injured.

If they know Luke slashed me and that's how I hurt my wrist, I see no reason why they wouldn't give me a second chance to make the team, Logan thought as Coach Vixen continued to look through his cluttered workspace.

Logan was temped to ask Coach Vixen straight up if they were going to give him another chance to make the team, possibly at next year's prospect tryout. But Coach

The Hockey Farmer

Vixen spoke before he had a chance, and Logan decided to keep his mouth shut.

"Here you go, kid," said the coach as he handed Logan the team list for the day, which Logan noticed was a lot shorter than the day before.

"Made some cuts, eh," said Logan, skimming through the list to see who was remaining on the roster.

"Yeah, we had a meeting with management early this morning and after several hours, we finally came to some decisions," said Coach Vixen. "I can tell you this was not an easy process at all—it was actually harder than it usually is." The Coach stretched out his arms in the air and yawned like a restless little baby.

Logan wasn't really paying attention to what Coach Vixen was saying, as he was now looking at the new roster list carefully. Logan noticed that Jack Patel's name was missing from the team list, as was Brent Jackson's. Logan thought there had been some sort of mistake and Brent's name had been left off the list inadvertently.

"Hey Coach, Brent's name isn't on this list," said Logan as if asking a question.

"Yeah, that was the decision we debated the most," said Coach Vixen. "We all agreed that he is a fantastic hockey player, but in the new National Hockey League that relies so much on speed and agility, we thought that his lack of mobility would prove to be his downfall." He'd obviously given a lot of thought to the matter.

Logan was stunned.

"Uhh, does he know?" asked Logan as he wondered how Brent would take the news.

"Not yet, and we would like to keep in that way for now," Coach Vixen replied sternly.

"But they're all getting changed right now for practice, aren't they?" asked Logan.

"Yeah, these decisions aren't actually completely set in stone. The players who are not on the list have this one practice to do something completely out of the ordinary to impress us and change our minds—but that isn't very likely," responded Coach Vixen.

Logan was still stunned.

"You better get up to the press box, kid, before we get this baby going," said Coach Vixen as he noticed that Logan wasn't thinking too clearly.

"Uhh, right," replied Logan as he finally took his eyes off the shortened list and left the coach's office.

Logan was tempted to find Brent Jackson and tell him that he needed to have the best practice of his life or else he was pretty much out of luck. But once again, he didn't want to do anything that would jeopardize his friendly relationship with Coach Vixen.

For the second day in a row, while up in the press box jotting down statistics and notes about his teammates, all Logan could think about was his short time with Samantha yesterday at Stanley Park and how they'd parted with a somewhat intimate yet G-rated hug. Logan had never felt this way about a girl before. He had only met Samantha a few days ago, and now he couldn't get her off his mind, and he was counting down the minutes until he would get to see her again after practice. It was a blessing in disguise of sorts that Logan had gotten injured, because he wasn't sure he would be able to completely focus on hockey now that he had met Samantha.

In addition, Logan was hoping that Brent would do something special to catch the eye of Coach Vixen and the

The Hockey Farmer

Vancouver Canucks' management, but it didn't seem like he did. It wasn't that Brent played badly; Logan thought he actually played fairly well, but judging from what Coach Vixen had told him prior to the practice, fairly well simply wouldn't cut it. It was actually a pretty sloppy and sluggish practice, which could have possibly been attributed to the fact that half the team was in all likelihood still nursing a hangover from the previous night. From Logan's perspective, no one really stood out for whatever reason. And for Brent Jackson and the rest of the players left off the updated team roster, that only meant one thing.

Chapter 19

"Logan!" yelled Samantha as she saw Logan walking across the street from Stanley Park, where they'd planned to meet for the second day in a row. "Over here!" she called as Logan looked around to see where the voice was coming from.

This time, it was Logan who was late rather than Samantha, but he had a pretty good reason why. After a fairly uneventful and disappointing practice, Coach Vixen had informed all of the players left off the team list that they had been released from the team. Logan had been back at the hotel, saying his goodbyes to all the players and exchanging contact information with a few others. Jack Patel would be heading back to the University of Minnesota, and of course Brent, was heading back to his parents' home here in Vancouver before he left for Ladner. Ladner was a suburb of Vancouver; it was also where his Vancouver Giants of the Western Hockey League would be holding their training camp this season.

"Oh, that's okay, don't worry about it," Samantha said as Logan explained why he was a little late for their rendezvous at the ice cream parlour by the side of Stanley Park. "So how was taking notes for the coach again?" she asked as they entered the shop.

The Hockey Farmer

"Oh, it was fantastic. I wish I could do that all the time instead of playing," Logan said sarcastically as he smiled and Samantha giggled.

"How was work?" Logan asked. "How long before you have to go back?" he added before Samantha had the chance to answer his original question.

"It was alright—the morning practice isn't too bad, because I just have to talk to the Coach and one or two players to get some interviews, and that's about it," responded Samantha, referring to the morning practice of the B.C. Lions football team. "I have to head back in a couple hours to watch the game so I can think of some questions to ask the players afterwards—now that's when it gets pretty crazy."

"I'm sure you can hold your own. At least I know you did after our practice, when the dressing room was crawling with reporters."

Samantha flashed her glowing smile at Logan once again, sending a shiver down his spine. "Thanks. I would invite you to come and watch with me, but I have to sit in the press box, and we're not allowed to bring anyone up with us," she added with regret.

"That's okay. I think I've seen enough of the press box anyways," responded Logan.

Samantha chuckled. "But if you wanted, you could buy a cheap ticket and bring some of your friends from the Canucks down to the game, and maybe we could meet up and do something after," she added. "But only if you want to." She flashed her radiant smile at Logan yet again.

"That doesn't sound like a bad idea," answered Logan, unable to resist Samantha's smile, which he had suddenly become very accustomed to. "I never thought that I would say that to a city girl," he teased as he smiled back at Samantha.

"Oh, shut up," Samantha said as she attempted to push Logan playfully, but Logan displayed his quick reflexes and caught both of her hands and didn't let go.

Logan quickly loosened up his grip on Samantha's hands to make sure he wasn't frightening her and continued to hold them tenderly. He then focused his attention to Samantha's beautiful blue eyes. Samantha looked right back at Logan; she appeared to be responding encouragingly to Logan's first move. Samantha smiled at Logan, and she seemed to be waiting for him to escalate the moment of gentle intimacy. Logan slowly leaned his head towards Samantha's, and she started to do the same. At that moment, before anything happened, Logan and Samantha's first romantic moment was broken by Samantha's Avril Lavigne ring-tone. Samantha was a huge Avril Lavigne fan, and Logan didn't mind her music either—but at that time, "so much for my happy ending" was the last thing either of them wanted to hear.

Samantha stopped moving her head towards Logan's and looked back into his eyes but didn't make the move to her cell phone, as she was rather embarrassed. Logan decided to make the well-mannered and considerate move.

"Go ahead and answer it—it could be important," he said respectfully, yet obviously discouraged.

"I'm so sorry, Logan," said Samantha as she pulled her phone out of her jeans pocket.

"Don't be," said Logan. He could clearly tell that Samantha already felt really bad about what just happened,

The Hockey Farmer

and being the gentleman he was, Logan didn't want to do or say anything that would make her feel even worse.

After a short conversation, Samantha looked at Logan and appeared to be even more disappointed and embarrassed than before, if that was even possible. "I'm so sorry, Logan," she said once again as she looked up at Logan for a second, and took her frustration out on her cell phone by slamming it shut with passion.

"I couldn't help but overhear your conversation; it sounded work related," Logan said calmly.

"Yes, it was. Supposedly the Lions made a pretty big trade, and they're holding a press conference at BC Place in about fifteen minutes to officially announce it. And guess what? I need to be there," responded Samantha, clearly disappointed.

"Well, you better get going then, eh," said Logan cheerfully, trying to raise Samantha's spirits.

Samantha didn't move.

"Come on, I'll walk you to your car," said Logan as he put his arm around Samantha's shoulders and started to walk towards the Stanley Park parking lot.

"Thanks for being so cool about this." Samantha pulled her keys out of her other pocket as she and Logan reached her car.

"You don't need to thank me." Reluctantly, Logan took his arm off of Samantha's shoulders in a subdued manner. "You have a good thing going on here, and I wouldn't want to mess it up for you," he added genuinely.

"I don't know what to say," said Samantha. She wanted Logan to know she really appreciated what he was doing but she didn't know how to express it in words.

"You don't have to say anything," responded Logan.

"I feel really bad just bailing on you two days in a row." Samantha took a seat in her car and put her in keys in the ignition.

"Don't worry. I know it's not your fault; you'd better get going or else you'll be late."

Samantha didn't want to leave Logan all alone, but she knew she had to. However, she still wanted to say something to Logan before she left that would show her appreciation. Typically, Samantha never had a problem coming up with words—she was a sports reporter, after all—but this time she couldn't think of anything that would express her sincere gratitude to Logan. *I guess actions speak louder than words anyway*, she thought as she jumped up out of her car.

Samantha took a deep breath and, without hesitation, kissed Logan gently yet affectionately near—but not on—the lips.

"Thank you for everything," she said as she got back into her car, flashed her sparkling smile at Logan, and then drove away.

"No, thank you," said Logan under his breath as he started to walk back to the hotel.

Even though Logan and Samantha's date had been cut short again, Logan was still rather pleased with it. And for the second day in a row, Logan couldn't get his mind off how their date had ended. He couldn't help but wonder how their date would end the next time they decided to go out.

Logan walked back to the hotel and pushed the elevator button to go back up to his room. The door opened shortly after, and Logan expected to see Luke Brown just like he had almost every other day. But instead he saw Frank Dempster, who was pretty much Logan's only friend left among the players now that Brent Jackson was gone.

"Oh good, Logan, I was looking for you," said Frank as he held the elevator door open.

"What's up?" asked Logan, curious.

"A couple of the guys are going to the Lions game tonight. You want to come?" Logan remembered he hadn't really confirmed with Samantha whether he was going to go to the game or not.

"Yeah, man, that would be sweet," he said excitedly. "Are we just going to get the tickets at the door or what?"

"I'm actually going to go run to the 7-11 right now—they have a deal going on, two tickets for $40 or something like that."

"Oh, do you want me to come with you?"

"No, don't worry about it; you'll probably slow me down anyways," Frank joked, and Logan was somewhat relieved he could go upstairs and just relax in his room for a couple of hours. "Pay me back later," added Frank as he finally let go of the elevator door and proceeded to run out of the hotel lobby as if he were preparing to run an Olympic 100-meter sprint.

Logan went up to his room and jumped into bed. He was surprisingly tired, even though he hadn't really done anything physically demanding in the past few days. It was ironic that earlier in the summer, when Logan had been in Cochrane filling his long days with hard and physically demanding work on the farm, he'd had trouble getting to sleep; now in Vancouver, all he was doing was taking notes for the coach and going out with Samantha, and he was constantly tired. It appeared the combined mental and emotional strain of hockey, Samantha, and just generally adjusting to staying on his own in a new city was taking a toll on Logan.

Before he even had a chance to ponder the many thoughts in his mind, Logan passed out on his bed, fully clothed, and began to snore heartily.

Chapter 20

"Samantha McMillan," said Logan to the well-toned security guard at BC Place during the half time of the B.C. Lions game.

"Samantha who?" asked the man.

"Samantha McMillan," Logan repeated.

"Sorry kid, never heard of her," said the security guard, denying Logan access to the elevator to the press box to meet Samantha.

"No one without a media pass is allowed up there anyway, so unless you have one in your pocket, just beat it," added the security guard with a stern look on his face.

Who are you, Michael Jackson? thought Logan as he turned around and started to walk back to where he and the others were sitting.

Logan tried to call Samantha on her cell phone several times, but to no avail. Logan would have at the very least liked to exchange pleasantries with Samantha and maybe get the opportunity to introduce her to Frank if he couldn't hang out with her, but neither of the two would be possible if he was unable to talk to her on the phone or in person.

"Any luck?" asked Frank as Logan returned to his seat.

"Nah, man. They wouldn't let me go up to the press box, and she's not picking up her phone," answered Logan as Luke Brown, who was sitting two seats away from Frank, listened in on their conversation.

"Oh well, I'm sure she's pretty busy up there anyways," said Frank, noticing Logan was somewhat upset.

"Yeah." Logan focused his attention on the playing field, where the players started to come back out of the dressing room for the second half.

"Hey, Watter, so you already got dumped by your girl after like two days, eh, sport?" said Luke Brown loudly enough that Logan could hear him over the roar of the crowd.

Logan decided to ignore him.

"What was the problem, not man enough for her?" yelled Luke as he and his two friends laughed boisterously.

Logan continued to watch the field and pretend he couldn't hear what Luke was saying.

"Don't take it personally, man. She just needs a real man; maybe you should give her my number?" added Luke.

Frank had heard enough and jumped to his feet in anger.

"What, now that Jackson's gone, is Dempster your new playmate?" yelled Luke. "What are you gonna do about it, Dempster, fight me?" Luke and his friends laughed out loud.

Frank made a move towards Luke, but Logan grabbed Frank's arms and held him back. "Frank!" he yelled. "He's not worth it!"

Frank peered over at Luke and then sat back down.

The Hockey Farmer

"Yeah that's what I thought, Dempster. Sit back down, son, maybe go buy a Nanaimo bar or something," yelled Luke as he and his friends continued to laugh obnoxiously.

Frank looked over to Logan.

"Sorry, man, no one insults my hometown," said Frank.

"Frank, wai—," responded Logan, but before he could finish Frank got up, leaned over Zach Campbell, who was sitting right next to him, and punched Luke smack in the face.

Before Luke had the chance to swing back at Frank, the B.C. Place security guards, who were conveniently already surveying the section, immediately intervened and escorted Frank out of the building. Since Logan could care less about football, since he couldn't get a hold of Samantha, and since he felt somewhat responsible for Frank's careless actions, Logan decided to follow Frank and the security guards out of the building.

"See ya later, children, have a nice night!" yelled Luke Brown as Logan and Frank left the seating area in the stadium accompanied by three B.C. Place security guards.

"What are you two looking at?" asked Luke, as his two friends seemed to be staring at him excessively.

"Uhh, you're bleeding, man," said one of them.

"Should be a nice shiner in the morning," said the other jokingly as Luke grunted and got up to wipe his face clean.

Meanwhile, Logan and Frank returned to the hotel after getting off with simply a warning from the security guards.

"That was pretty stupid, you know, Frank," said Logan as he and Frank entered the Fairmont Hotel's lobby.

"Yeah, I know," answered Frank as he and Logan both chuckled. "But you have to admit, I got him pretty good, didn't I?" he added as he and Logan entered the elevator.

"Buddy, that was beautiful. Where did you learn to fight like that?"

"The BCHL, man. It may not be the most skilled league, but it's definitely one of the feistiest," responded Frank, referring to the British Columbia Hockey League, where he played on the Nanaimo Clippers. "I'm going to get to bed, man. Last day tomorrow; I gotta make a good impression."

"Alright, take it easy," replied Logan as he and Frank went their separate ways.

Even though he didn't show it, Logan was kind of caught off-guard by what Frank had just said. Since he really wasn't paying much attention to the hockey aspect of his trip anymore, Logan hadn't realized that tomorrow was the last day of the tryout, and he would be heading back home to Cochrane the day after. His feelings were all over the place. Logan was looking forward to going back home to his father and the farm and once again sleeping in his own bed. But on the other hand, he was starting to enjoy the life he had here in Vancouver, and he was *really* starting to enjoy whatever it was that he had going on with Samantha.

Logan took a quick shower and then jumped into bed and turned on the television. He quickly put it on channel 30, hoping to catch a glimpse of Samantha in the post-game coverage in the dressing room of the B.C. Lions game. However, he was disappointed to see they were actually showing more Major League Baseball playoff highlights. Logan glanced over to his alarm clock to check the time. It was 10:30. *The game must have ended about half an hour ago*, Logan thought as he flipped through the other channels.

Lo and behold, even though Logan was tempted to call it a night, he decided to put on Channel 24 and watch some more re-runs of *The OC*. Oddly enough for a hockey player growing up on a farm in Alberta, Logan was always really into the "chick flicks" and drama-packed teenage series, and that was precisely what "The O.C." was. And that was why Logan loved it so much.

Oh, what a classic, Logan thought as he realized Much Music was airing the episode where Marissa shot Trey, the brother of her boyfriend Ryan.

As Logan put down the remote on his bedside table and got comfortable in his bed, preparing for a couple hours of nothing but *The OC*, his Backstreet Boys ring-tone went off. Logan groaned as he leaned over towards his bedside table to grab his cell. *Who would be calling me at this time?* he wondered.

"Hello?"

"Hey, Logan, it's Samantha," she said as Logan jumped up in delight and re-arranged himself into a more comfortable position for talking.

"Oh, hey, how's it going?" asked Logan.

"I'm alright, just got back home from the Lions game."

"How did it go?"

"It wasn't that great. Just another day on the job, I guess," said Samantha as she and Logan shared a little chuckle.

"So, I called you a few times during the game," said Logan, wondering if Samantha knew he was actually at the game.

"I just saw that after the game, and that's why I called you," she said. Logan was somewhat disappointed that Samantha had only called him to return his missed calls.

"I actually left my purse and my cell phone in the press box when I went down to the dressing rooms at half time, and it turns out I didn't get to go back up to the press box until the game was over," added Samantha. Logan realized that Samantha hadn't even been up in the press box when he'd tried to meet her there at half time.

"I'm so sorry about that and about bailing on you the past two days," added Samantha sincerely.

"Oh, don't worry about it; it's no big deal," said Logan, trying to downplay what had happened.

"Well, it's a big deal to me, and it's a big deal how cool you were about everything. I just want you to know how much I appreciate it."

"Uhh, well, then I guess I should say you're welcome," said Logan as Samantha giggled.

"So what were the three missed calls all about?" she asked, enthusiastically changing the subject.

"Well, I was actually calling you to find out where you were so we could maybe meet up somewhere in the stadium."

"Oh my God, you came to the game?"

"Sure did."

The Hockey Farmer

"Well that's just great. Now I feel even worse for not picking up the phone. What a bad day."

"Samantha, cheer up!" said Logan passionately. "Don't even worry about it—I was only there until early in the third quarter anyways."

"You left early? You gotta be kidding me."

"Well, I left early, but I didn't exactly leave willingly."

"Oh my God, Logan, what did you do?"

"Well, it was pretty complicated," responded Logan, trying to make sure Samantha actually wanted to know what happened instead of just trying to be polite by asking about his day.

"Well, I'm listening," said Samantha.

"Are you sure you want to hear it? It's not even that great of a story."

"Well, if it's about you, I'm sure I'll like it. Now tell me!" yelled Samantha into her phone.

"Fine," Logan said sternly, having finally determined that Samantha legitimately wanted to hear about his day.

Logan proceeded to tell Samantha how Luke had taunted him and Frank, and then how Frank had finally taken exception to Luke's constant abuse by punching him in the face. After that, Logan and Samantha continued to talk about a variety of things, including their respective families and lives while growing up. They soon realized that they came from very different families and lifestyles, but that didn't seem to bother them one bit. However, lacking from their wide range of conversation topics was Logan's return flight to Cochrane, which was the day after tomorrow. Logan wanted to tell Samantha he would soon be leaving the beautiful city of Vancouver, but he didn't want to ruin the pleasant conversation they were having, so he decided not to tell her, at least not that night. Before they knew it, Logan and Samantha had been talking on the phone for almost two hours. Since it was one in the morning and both of them had to wake up fairly early the next morning, and considering their respective phone bills, Logan and Samantha decided to call it a night.

"It was nice talking to you," said Samantha.

"And once again, I'm really sorr—" added Samantha as Logan interrupted her before she had the chance to apologize for what seemed to Logan like the millionth time of the day.

"You better not say you're sorry. I've heard enough of that word for one day."

"Good night, Logan," said Samantha as she obliged with Logan's wishes.

"Good night."

Chapter 21

Before the last practice the next morning, Coach Aaron Vixen and assistant General Manager Sean Townsend called a team meeting to discuss how many players they would be bringing along from this prospects tryout to the main Vancouver Canucks training camp. Logan and most of the others assumed they would only bring along two or three players to the main training camp, which would be held in Victoria, because that was how many players they had usually brought along in the years past. The players were uncertain whether Coach Vixen and Sean Townsend were actually going to use this meeting to inform the group which players made the cut, so to speak, or if it was just to let them know how many players they planned on bringing along.

"Hey Frank, I'll tell you right now that they're only going to take you and Luke back to Victoria," said Logan as he and Frank walked to the conference room of the Fairmont Hotel after breakfast.

"Honestly, if they take me, I don't care who else they bring," said Frank. "Playing in my province for the Vancouver Canucks; can't get much better than that." Frank's hometown of Nanaimo was a small city about two hours away from Victoria.

"But you have to admit, it would be pretty awkward if they only took you and Luke. You know, considering what happened last night."

"Well, how about this: if you're right and they only decide to bring Luke and me along, I won't walk alone on the ferry ride to Victoria." As Frank spoke, he and Logan entered the conference room and took their seats near the back of the fairly large room.

As the players trickled into the conference room, Frank was only waiting to see Luke Brown to see if he had any marks from last night's events. While Frank would have loved to see Luke with a first class shiner, he still hoped that Luke's face was fine because he didn't want any of the coaches to start asking any questions. Luckily, as Luke entered the room soon after, Frank noticed that his face wasn't actually that bad. There was a fairly noticeable mark; however, it was far from a black eye, and it wasn't something that would raise any suspicions from the coaches—or anyone else, for that matter.

"Man, I thought he would definitely have a black eye. I guess I'm not as tough as I thought," Frank whispered to Logan as Coach Vixen and Sean Townsend entered the room once all the players were already present.

"He's probably wearing makeup," whispered Logan back to Frank as they both laughed quietly.

Luke Brown stared at Frank and Logan as he heard them whispering; at the same time, Coach Vixen started talking.

"This is it, boys: The last couple hours you have to show us what you're really made of. I don't want to see anyone slacking off today, because as Sean is about to inform you, a lot of you still have a chance to make the trip

The Hockey Farmer

to Victoria with the big boys," said Coach Vixen as Logan and all the others wondered what the Coach was talking about. "Make the most of it, guys. Don't take anything for granted, because this last practice could determine where you play hockey this year and in the future. That's all from me; Sean, you want to take over?" finished Coach Vixen. The players waited attentively to hear what Sean was about to say.

"Alright, boys, I'm going to keep this nice and short. As of right now, we have only decided on one player who will be coming to Victoria with us for sure," said Sean Townsend as a wave of disappointment and curiosity took over the conference room. "But we have an eye on a lot of you, and for that reason, the coaching staff and I decided that we will be bringing five of you along for the ride to the main Vancouver Canucks camp." A wave of excitement and curiosity now took over the room. "After today's practice, we're going to have some meetings with the coaching staff and scouts to see where everyone stands, and after that, we will let you know which of you will be coming along," Sean went on. "But that won't be for a few days, so all of you will be going back home tomorrow, and then we'll go from there." Logan was still sure about Frank and Luke, but he wondered who the other three players would be.

"Good luck, boys; let's get going to the arena," said Sean as he and Coach Vixen got up and left the room, closely followed by the rest of the players.

"Five players, eh? Maybe you do have a chance, Logan," Frank teased, not realizing that Luke Brown was right behind the two of them, once again listening in on their conversation, as all the players entered the bus on its way to General Motors Place for the last time.

Logan laughed.

"Nah, I don't think so, Dempster. They would need to take half of this city if Watter wanted to come with us," said Luke Brown as he continued to focus on tormenting Logan, even though Frank was the one who'd punched him last night.

"Who said you're going?" asked Logan, even though he was positive that Luke was going to be one of the five players who made the trip to the island.

"I always go, Watter," responded Luke.

"And yet you always get cut and end up back here at prospects camp, don't you?" said Frank.

Luke ignored Frank and took his seat on the bus.

When the group arrived at General Motors Place, it was business as usual. But everyone including the players, coaches, management and training staff seemed to have increased their level of intensity by a couple of notches. Luke would usually make some smug comments in the dressing room as the players got changed, but this time even he seemed to be focusing on the task at hand. Since many of the players, including Brent Jackson and Jack Patel, had been released from the team, there was no need to split up the group into two on-ice sessions. This time, every single player would hit the ice first together, and then after that, they would hit the training facility together.

Much to Logan's contentment, he wouldn't have to go up into the lowly press box and take notes for Coach Vixen this time around. He had another appointment with John Stevenson, the team's doctor, to get a final verdict on his injured wrist. While Logan was pleased he wouldn't

The Hockey Farmer

have to take notes for the Coach today, he was somewhat disappointed that he wouldn't be able to watch the team's practice—judging by the intensity and focus level of every single player in the dressing room, it had all the makings of a good one.

"How does this feel?" asked team doctor John Stevenson as he pressed down on Logan's wrist.

"It feels fine, just like normal," responded Logan truthfully.

"How about this?" asked the doctor as he pressed Logan's wrist in a different position.

Logan grumbled in pain. "Not great," he responded, disappointed that his wrist was still not fully healed.

"Alright, that's actually normal," said the doctor, and Logan was somewhat relieved.

"Everything looks to be right on schedule. Unless we encounter any major setbacks in the next day or two, you should be ready to play again in no more than five days," added the doctor enthusiastically.

"I can live with that," said Logan as he swiftly got up and left the medical room, making his way into the stands so he could catch the last half of the team practice.

Logan was surprised to see Sean Townsend sitting a couple of rows behind the penalty box in the stands, so he decided to join him.

"How's the wrist coming along?" asked Sean as he continued to watch what was happening on the ice.

"It's pretty good. The doctor says it will be fully healed in a maximum of five days," answered Logan as he took a seat next to Sean.

"Good to hear," responded Sean as he shuffled through the papers in his binder. On the ice, Zach Campbell had just scored a beautiful goal on an end-to-end rush similar to Logan's earlier in the week.

Just as Logan had expected, the practice was very intense. A few minutes after Logan took his seat; the team split up into two groups and started to play a scrimmage for the last twenty minutes of the ice time. If Logan didn't know any better, judging by the aggressive play and high level of intensity, he would have thought that this was the Stanley Cup Finals rather than simply a prospects tryout scrimmage. It wasn't hard to tell that Frank Dempster and Luke Brown were the cream of the crop out there. They were always first to the puck and always seemed to make the right plays with or without the puck, while maintaining their proper position. But aside from Frank and Luke, Logan didn't really see anyone else who stood out during the scrimmage, so he was still fairly surprised that the team would be taking five players to the main camp.

For the first time all week, Logan was actually somewhat tempted to stay at the arena and watch some more hockey rather than go hang out with Samantha. It wasn't that he didn't enjoy her company; on the contrary, he truly took pleasure in talking to her and spending time with her. And he had no problem at all with looking at her either. It was just that Logan was dreading the conversation he would inevitably have with her about returning to Cochrane the following day. He was just starting to get close to her, both physically and emotionally, and he didn't want that to change. Logan wanted their relationship to continue to develop, as he felt it had the potential to be something special, and he didn't want to say or do anything

The Hockey Farmer

that would put the happiness they might share in the future at risk.

I have to talk to her. I just can't leave without saying goodbye, Logan thought as the scrimmage came to an end and all the players left the ice. *But how? How do I tell her I'm leaving just when we're starting to get to know each other?* he wondered as he drowned himself in his thoughts. *I'm sure she'll understand; she knows I have to go back and help my dad,* Logan went on, remembering he'd talked to Samantha about his father and the farm during their phone conversation. *But what if she just forgets about me? She probably has a bunch of guys lining up to step in and take my place.*

What is my place, anyways? said a voice in Logan's mind.

At that moment, Logan heard Sean Townsend say something, but he was too lost in his thoughts to comprehend what he'd said.

"Uh, sorry, what was that?" asked Logan as his cheeks began to turn a rosy pink.

"I said, have something on your mind?" repeated Sean.

"Uh, yeah, just drowning in my sorrow about how I could have been out there competing instead of watching from the sidelines." The answer was somewhat true, even if he hadn't been thinking about that at that exact moment in time.

Sean chuckled. "Just keep working hard, and I'm sure you'll get to where you eventually want to be," he said. Logan, meanwhile, tried to analyze his response and judge what his comments really meant.

"Alright, I'm going to head upstairs and talk to Don. Take care, kid," added Sean as he closed his binder and left the seating area.

Don Gale was the President and General Manager of the Vancouver Canucks. Logan had actually never met him—he always dealt with rookies through either Coach Vixen or Sean—but from everything others told him about Don, he was the ultimate competitor, and he would always stand with and defend his team. Logan hoped he would have the chance to meet Don sometime in the near future for the simple reason that rookies only got to meet the General Manager if they were signing a contract with the team.

Right at the same time Logan got up and made his way down to the dressing rooms to talk to Frank and some of the other guys, his cell phone went off. Logan assumed Samantha would be the one who was calling him.

"Hello," he said.

"Hey Logan, I can't talk for long because I'm on my lunch break."

Just as Logan had thought, it was Samantha. "Hey, what's up?" he asked coolly.

"Oh, not too much. I just wanted to make sure that we're still on for dinner later this evening," Samantha said with her innocent and soothing voice.

"Uhh, yeah, for sure."

"I'll pick you up at five, alright?" asked Samantha as she giggled.

"Sure. So I guess you're the man in this relationship, eh?" After Samantha's short pause, he quickly realized he had said the word "relationship."

Samantha giggled again.

"Okay. I have to go, Logan, see you tonight!" Samantha said enthusiastically as she hung up the phone.

"Ughh, women," Logan said under his breath as he too hung up the phone and made his way down to the dressing rooms.

Chapter 22

Logan came down to the hotel lobby at 4:59 with Frank Dempster, who was going to meet some members of his family for dinner. They both saw Samantha pulling into the visitors' parking lot, sporting her beautiful black Honda Civic.

"Damn," said Frank excitedly as Logan wondered what was wrong.

"What's up?" asked Logan earnestly.

"Oh," responded Frank, acting as if he were surprised. "Just tell me how that leather interior feels when you get back tonight, if you know what I mean," Frank teased as he came out the hotel door with Logan and then walked towards the bus stop.

"Oh, shut your mouth and go back to Nanaimo, Dempster," Logan joked as he walked towards Samantha's parked car.

Logan hopped into Samantha's car, they exchanged pleasantries, and she drove off from the hotel as Logan waved at Frank, who was still waiting at the bus stop,

"You know we could just give him a ride wherever he needs to go, right?" said Samantha as Logan waved at Frank at the bus stop.

"Oh that's alright. He's going to some place which starts with Port, and he said it's pretty far from here."

The Hockey Farmer

"Port Coquitlam?" asked Samantha.

"I don't think so," Logan responded uncertainly.

"Must be Port Moody, then."

"That's the one. Like, how am I supposed to remember a name like Port Moody?" Logan asked sarcastically.

"You're not; that's why I'm here," responded Samantha as she took her eyes off the road for a second and flashed her first smile of the night towards Logan.

Logan didn't actually know where Samantha was taking him, but he wasn't really concerned about that. All he could think about was how to tell her that he was leaving the next morning and how she would take in the news.

"What are you thinking about?" asked Samantha. She'd noticed that something was on Logan's mind, seeing as he hadn't said a word in the past several minutes.

Oh God, should I tell her? Logan wondered. *No, I can't tell her now. I'll wait until dinner*, Logan set his mind at rest.

"Uhh, no, nothing too important," Logan lied.

Samantha was not fooled.

"Logan, even though we haven't spent that much time together, I can still tell that you're thinking about something, and I would really appreciate it if you were honest with me." Samantha's disappointed voice was similar to that of parents giving a child the talk where they're not mad, but let down.

Logan didn't want to keep lying to Samantha, but he didn't want to break the news to her while she was driving, either.

"Uhh, alright, I'm just thinking about what could have been with the Canucks," responded Logan, once again not entirely stretching out the truth.

"Care to elaborate at all?" asked Samantha as she stopped at a red light and looked over towards Logan.

"Well, it's just that I had such a great opportunity to make the team this week, and I got injured before I even had the chance to make an impression. I can't help but wonder if this was the last chance I had to make the big leagues, and I just blew it," added Logan as Samantha listened attentively.

"Logan, you can't think that way," said Samantha as the traffic light turned green and she refocused her attention to the road.

Logan remained silent.

"If it's meant to be then it's meant to be, Logan. You can't stress it," added Samantha. Logan continued to remain silent, so she went on. "And anyways, it wasn't even your fault you got injured. How were you supposed to protect yourself from getting slashed on the wrist?"

"Well, some of the guys did warn me that Luke Brown had a screw loose. But you're right; I need to stop worrying about spilled milk," said Logan. "Did I just say I need to stop worrying about spilled milk?" he added, embarrassed.

"I think you did, unfortunately," answered Samantha as she laughed out loud. "Alright, we're here." She pulled into the parking lot of a fancy-looking Italian cuisine restaurant on Robson Street.

Robson Street was one of the busiest and most popular streets in all of Vancouver, let alone in the downtown area. The restaurant, the Caffe de Medici, had

The Hockey Farmer

been up and running for a grand total of twenty-five years, due to its assortment of delicious food, drink, and elegant indoor and patio dining. Dining at such an exquisite restaurant was far from a regularity for Logan. He could precisely remember the last time he ate at a fancy restaurant: A few years ago at his aunt and uncle's 20th wedding anniversary, held at an upscale Chinese restaurant in downtown Calgary. On the other hand, Samantha and her family had a sit-down meal at the Caffe de Medici once a week, at the very least.

    Samantha ordered a roasted chicken dish with rosemary, lemon and garlic, while Logan ordered a classic dish of fettuccine alfredo, which was one of the only items he recognized on the whole menu. Logan was actually enjoying this nice little dinner with Samantha, and by her overall demeanour, he could tell she felt the same way—which made it even harder for Logan to break the news to her that he'd be leaving bright and early the next morning. But as their respective meals arrived, Logan decided he couldn't wait any longer. He would have to tell her, and he would have to tell her now.

    Oh, what the hell, the right time isn't ever going to come anyways, Logan thought as he took a deep breath, took a forkful of his fettuccine alfredo, took a sip of his peach-flavoured iced tea, and prepared himself to tell Samantha the truth.

    "Samantha, I need to talk to you," said Logan as he guzzled his tall glass of iced tea.

    "Haven't we been talking for the past hour or so?" asked Samantha for a laugh.

    Logan didn't laugh; he remained silent. Samantha could tell something was bothering him deep inside.

"What's wrong, Logan?" she asked with concern.

"I'm going back home to Cochrane tomorrow morning," said Logan finally, without any hesitation.

This time, it was Samantha that remained silent.

"The Canucks booked my ticket for me at the start of the week, and now that the tryout is over, I really have to get back home."

Samantha took a sip of her water.

"I'm sorry for not telling you earlier, but I didn't want to ruin the last couple of days we had together," added Logan honestly.

"You don't have to explain yourself to me," responded Samantha, evidently in disbelief.

"But what if I want to?" asked Logan.

"It's okay, Logan. I get it and I understand it," responded Samantha as she attempted to take another sip of water, but realized her glass was empty.

Logan took another bite of his fettuccine alfredo, and Samantha did the same with her rosemary chicken. After about a minute of pure silence, aside from the chewing of their food and sipping of their drinks, Logan spoke up.

"We'll definitely keep in touch, right?"

"Yeah, of course we will, Logan," answered Samantha as she finally looked up at Logan and flashed her beautiful smile at him. "Oh, and don't worry—we'll be seeing a lot more of each other." Logan wondered what she was implying.

"Oh yeah, and how is that?"

"Well, once you make the Canucks, you'll have to find a place to live here in Vancouver, and you'll be

The Hockey Farmer

spending a lot of time at General Motors Place. And lucky for you, I spend a lot of my time there, too."

"I like your optimism," Logan said.

"Oh, nice word, 'optimism.' I thought I was supposed to be the smart one in this relationship," said Samantha, instantly realizing she'd classified herself and Logan as being in a "relationship" for the first time.

From there on out, much to both Logan and Samantha's delight, their conversation went back to normal, just as it had been before Logan broke the news. They decided they would forget about the past and the future and just focus on the present. They stayed true to their word. After dinner, Logan and Samantha went back to Stanley Park for dessert, along with a late evening promenade around the park, just as they had done the previous two days. Both Logan and Samantha thoroughly took advantage of the rest of their night together, because despite Samantha's positive attitude, neither of them knew when they would see the other again.

Chapter 23

"Last call for all passengers for flight 585 to Calgary, Alberta," repeated the monotone-voiced PA announcer in the airport, which seemed identical to the announcer on Logan's first flight to Vancouver. But this time he was leaving the city with a much different perspective than he'd had before he stepped foot on British Columbian soil.

Just like the Calgary airport, Logan wasn't too familiar with YVR, the Vancouver airport. But this time around, Logan arrived at the airport much earlier than he really needed to, just so he could familiarize himself with the surroundings and make sure that he wasn't late for his flight again. Before Logan stepped foot onto the medium-sized plane, he took a look outside and wondered when he would return to this beautiful city, if he ever would again. He and Samantha hadn't really sorted out any of their issues last night, if you could even call them that. They'd put everything else aside and just enjoyed their last night together, which had felt like the right thing to do at the time. But the next morning, as Logan buckled his seatbelt on the plane en route back home to Cochrane, he kind of regretted not talking to Samantha about much more important things than music and movies—such as the state

The Hockey Farmer

of their relationship, or if they even had a relationship at all.

Logan passed out in his seat before the plane had even taken off. He hadn't slept much the previous night, and he knew he would have to immediately pick up his workload once he arrived back home at the farm—he wanted to finish re-establishing the farm as soon as possible so he could focus solely on hockey. Logan wasn't sure where he was going to play this upcoming season since he was now too old to play Midget hockey. He hadn't earned a contract with the Vancouver Canucks, but he was certain he wanted to play hockey somewhere. Logan decided to give Hunter, his previous Midget coach, a call right after he landed in Calgary—Logan remembered that Hunter had gotten someone to videotape almost every one of their games from the past two seasons. Logan thought the best way for him to find a place to play hockey this upcoming season was to make a DVD with an assortment of his top highlights from the past two seasons and start sending them to junior teams all over the Canadian Hockey League. The Western Hockey League was obviously Logan's first choice so he could stay relatively close to home, possibly even in Alberta for Calgary, Medicine Hat, Red Deer or Lethbridge, or maybe even in British Columbia for Vancouver or Chilliwack. But Logan wasn't going to limit himself to simply teams in the Western Hockey League; he would also send the DVD to teams in the Ontario or Quebec Hockey Leagues to make sure he gave himself a full opportunity to land a place to play for the upcoming season, which was quickly approaching. If he was unable to find himself a gig, Logan would be content to accept Hunter's offer and begin his career as a coach rather than a player.

"Sir," said the stewardess. The plane had landed in Calgary and Logan was still asleep.

Logan didn't respond.

"Sir," repeated the stewardess, this time just a little bit louder. All the other passengers had already exited the aircraft.

Logan still didn't respond; however, he did slightly change his position on the seat.

"Sir, wake up!" repeated the stewardess for the third time, this time even louder than the first two, as she nudged Logan's shoulder softly.

"Uhh, yeah?" Logan finally responded as he itched his eyes and acted as if he hadn't been in a deep sleep for the past couple hours.

"Well, for starters, you could get up and leave so I can start cleaning the plane and I can leave, too," responded the stewardess pleasantly, with a smile on her face that reminded Logan of Samantha's glowing grin.

Logan slid open his window and realized the plane was no longer in the air, and then he looked around him and noticed he was the only one left on the plane, aside from the plane crew themselves.

"Oh, uhh, sorry about that," said Logan, especially embarrassed since he was talking to a fairly good-looking woman, as he quickly got up and reached for his backpack from the storage department above his seat.

"Don't worry about it," replied the stewardess, clearly exhausted, as she laughed.

The Hockey Farmer

"We usually get a couple sleepers per day; it's nothing too out of the ordinary," she added as she helped Logan with his backpack.

"Thanks," said Logan politely as he smiled good-naturedly at the stewardess.

"No problem," replied the stewardess as she smiled right back at Logan, looking almost eerily indistinguishable from Samantha.

"Well, I better get going," Logan said, finally breaking the awkward eye contact and silence between the two of them.

"Yes, of course, have a nice day," replied the stewardess. "Oh, and thank you for flying with West Jet," added the stewardess politely as Logan chuckled and at last exited the plane.

W*omen*, Logan thought as he walked down the hallway and saw his father waiting for him, waving his hands furiously at the gate entrance located at the end of the corridor.

On the ride from Calgary to Cochrane, Jacob had many questions about Logan's experience in Vancouver, questions that Logan really wasn't too interested in answering, at least for the time being. For one, even with Logan's power nap on the airplane, he was still exhausted, so the only thing on his mind on the way back to Cochrane was sleep. Secondly, Logan was still debating whether or not he wanted to tell his father about Samantha. Logan wasn't the type of teenager who would keep things from his father. He had never done so in the past, nor did he want to start doing so now, but he didn't know what he had with Samantha, so he didn't know what to tell his father about her. So Logan decided to keep quiet on this matter, at least for the time being.

"So, did they say they would give you another chance?" asked Jacob as Logan opened his eyes and they entered the city of Cochrane. "You know, since you were injured and you didn't really get a fair chance to show what you got," he added—Logan had already told him about the injury earlier in the week via text message.

"Well, they told me they liked what they saw from me and would keep a close eye on me, but I don't know—they might just be saying that."

"I'm sure they meant it, but if they said they're going to keep a close eye on you, I guess you're going to have to find yourself somewhere to play, aren't you?" Obviously, Jacob had already given the subject some thought before his conversation with Logan.

"Oh, right—I was going to call Coach Hunter and ask him if we could come pick up some game film from the last few seasons so I can start sending it to some junior teams," Logan said as he pulled his cell phone from the side pocket of his backpack.

"Are you calling him right now?" asked Jacob as he saw Logan pulling out his phone.

"Uhh, yes," responded Logan without emotion.

"Well, you might want to rethink that, because I already called him," said Jacob pleasantly.

"Why would you call Coach Hunter?" asked Logan curiously, unable to put two and two together.

"You are my son, Logan; we do think alike," responded Jacob, but Logan still wasn't able to put his finger on what his father was trying to say. "I already got the game film, and I've already marked down which of the

The Hockey Farmer

games you scored a goal in," added Jacob with an immense smile on his face.

Logan was stunned.

"Wow, thanks, Dad, you didn't really nee—" said Logan as his father promptly interrupted him.

"I wanted to help you in any way I could, and besides, I need something to do at night when I'm not on the farm."

"Uhh, thanks, how is the farm coming along, anyways?" asked Logan, sparking some friendly conversation with his father to make sure he knew Logan appreciated what he had done for him.

"It's coming along. Obviously still have some work left to do, but with you back in the fold, we should be able to get'er done in no time," replied Jacob as he arrived home and pulled into the driveway.

"Awesome, glad to be back." Logan jumped out of the car and grabbed his suitcase from the trunk. "Oh and Dad—"

"Yes, Logan?"

"Don't ever say 'get'er done' again," Logan said, and he and his father both laughed loudly as they walked towards the house.

Chapter 24

The following day, it was back to work for Logan. He didn't really get a chance to take any downtime after his week-long trip to Vancouver—not because his father didn't allow him to do so, but because Logan wanted to jump right back onto the horse, so to speak, and get back to work as quickly as possible. Logan wanted to cherish these last few weeks of summer working on the farm because if everything worked out to plan, Logan would playing hockey again sooner rather than later, and he wouldn't have very much time to come back to the farm. But before Logan could even think about possibly landing a gig in the big leagues, he needed to land a gig in the juniors.

The previous night, Logan had spent a couple hours surfing the internet to see which teams in the Canadian Hockey League needed an offensive-minded forward and which teams he would like to play for. After some intensive research and exhaustive thinking, Logan narrowed his list down to twenty teams because, after all, he couldn't send out a DVD to every single team in the whole league. On Logan's list were ten teams from the Western Hockey League, five from the Ontario Hockey League, and five from the Quebec Hockey League. Logan decided he would head down to Canada Post after work and send out the copies of the DVD, and if he didn't hear from any of the teams within two weeks, he would start looking at the Alberta Junior Hockey League or the British Columbia Hockey League route, which was the same league that Frank Dempster played in. It was pretty safe to say that farming wasn't the main thing on Logan's mind when he went back to work the next morning.

"Logan, can you just wheel in the next batch from the storage room when you're done fixing that machine?" asked Jacob, referring to the next batch of eggs that needed to be brought into the grading station, as he and Logan worked feverishly in the grading station despite the scorching temperature outside.

"Yeah, sure," responded Logan as he focused on repairing the faulty grading equipment.

During Logan's absence, Jacob had maintained the farm quite nicely, and Logan didn't expect anything less coming from a blue-collar worker like his father. But the fact of the matter was that two people could get a lot more work done at a much faster rate than just one person, so Jacob had slightly fallen behind on the grading of the eggs—which Logan had also somewhat expected. But in his father's defence, the grading was the only aspect of the farm he had slightly slowed down on. Jacob had stayed on par with everything else: Checking the waters, milking the cows, farming the tractors, feeding the chickens, collecting their eggs, maintaining the barns, and looking after all the paperwork, which seemed to increase day by day. In addition, Jacob had hired someone to install a new upper echelon security system on the premises due to all the recent robberies of farms (of all places!) around the area in the last several weeks. After realizing all the work this father had done on the farm in the past few days, he began to appreciate his father making the game film even more than he already did.

How does this guy just keep on going and going? Logan wondered as he wheeled the next batch of eggs from the storage room to the grading station. *If he's strong enough to work on a farm every single day for thirty years, I surely can work hard enough to make the National Hockey League*, Logan thought as he began to unload all the cartons from the aged and rusted wheelbarrow-like transferring equipment they used at the farm. *Because after all, he is my father and we do share the same blood*, Logan went on as he remembered his father working tirelessly on the farm day in and day out without ever complaining one bit.

It was a fairly uneventful day on the farm for both Logan and Jacob. They started off the morning with the grading, which took a few hours longer than usual just so they could get back to their previous pace, and then they split off into their respective individual tasks. Jacob noticed that Logan had again considerably picked up his work ethic, while picking up his workload at the same time. Even though Jacob was proud to see his son working so hard, just like he had been preaching to him since the day he was born, he was also somewhat concerned. First of all, he didn't want Logan to aggravate his wrist injury which, despite what Logan said, was yet to be fully healed. And secondly, Jacob didn't want Logan to wear himself out working on the farm just to please him before the hockey season started. Staying true to his word was another of Logan's finest qualities, and it was another quality Jacob truly admired; however, Jacob also knew that sometimes Logan had the tendency to stay true to his word almost to a

The Hockey Farmer

fault. Jacob decided he would give Logan the benefit of the doubt, trusting that his son knew how hard he was able to push himself rather than confronting him. The last thing Jacob wanted to do was to start a war of words with his son when for all he knew, this would be the last few weeks he would spend with Logan before he moved out of the house, and quite possibly even out of the city when September rolled around.

    Logan finished up on the farm for the day, came back into the house to pick up the DVDs of his game film, and then went directly to Canada Post. Logan had written down the mailing addresses of all the teams on the packages the night before, so all he had to do was drop the twenty packages off at the outbox. Logan said a quick prayer before he entered the building, and then he sent the packages off a few minutes later after signing some papers at the front desk. When Logan got back home and took a seat on the rocking chair in his room, he soon realized he hadn't thought about Samantha once the whole day until this point, and he didn't know if that was a good sign or not. Most of Logan's attention throughout the day had been focused on work or hockey, just as it had been earlier in the summer, before he met Samantha.

    Logan secretly hoped that the Vancouver Giants, one of the teams Logan had sent a package to, would be the team he would end up on—for more than one reason. For one, Logan had heard many good things about their coach, Dave Hanson. He was a former National Hockey League coach and had the fantastic reputation of developing junior players into good, all-around professional hockey players. Secondly, the Vancouver Giants had won the Memorial Cup last season—at home in Vancouver, for that matter.

The Memorial Cup was widely considered to be the hardest trophy to win in all of sports, because it was rewarded to the top team out of the entire Canadian Hockey League, which consisted of the Western, Ontario and Quebec Leagues. And lastly, if Logan was signed by the Vancouver Giants, he would obviously have to move to Vancouver, and if that took place, he would undoubtedly see a lot more of Samantha. Logan didn't know what he wanted more: To see Samantha almost on a daily basis, or to play hockey with the defending Memorial Cup champions and on one of the most respected organizations in all of the Canadian Hockey League. Either way, he would relish the opportunity to do both.

As Logan hopped into bed that night, he wondered whether he should call Samantha. He knew it was probably the respectable and honourable thing to do, but he didn't know what he would say. Logan sat in his bed, staring at his light brown wall, once again regretting not having the relationship discussion with Samantha when he had the perfect opportunity to do so back in Vancouver.

Maybe I should just call her and figure out what's going on with us once and for all, Logan thought as he picked up his phone from his bedside table. *But... I don't want to push it and make it seem like I'm eager to jump into any sort of relationship.*

Oh, just make up your mind, would you, and let me go to sleep? said a voice in Logan's mind.

Logan decided that he would listen to the so-called voice of reason in his mind and call it a night. He plugged his phone into his charger on the bedside table, set his alarm clock, which currently displayed 10:30, for 7:00 the next morning, and slipped comfortably under his extra

The Hockey Farmer

warm light grey duvet cover. At the exact moment Logan closed his eyes, he was surprised and somewhat excited to hear his Backstreet Boys ring-tone go off. He reached over and picked up his phone as quickly as possible so that it wouldn't wake up his father, who was fast asleep in the next room.

"Hello," answered Logan, fairly certain who was on the other end of the phone line, as he sat up straight and leaned against his bedpost.

"Hi, Logan, it's me," Samantha said rather solemnly.

"Samantha, I was meaning to call you," Logan said in an apologetic tone of voice.

"How was your flight?" Samantha asked abruptly, getting the customary good-natured remarks out of the way.

"It was good, slept for the most part," responded Logan, doing the same.

"That's good," said Samantha.

"So did you get home okay?" asked Logan.

"Yeah, I was fine; there weren't many other cars on the road at that time anyway."

"That's good," Logan responded, mimicking Samantha, followed by an elongated silence.

"Logan," said Samantha.

"Yes?"

"We need to talk."

Logan prepared himself for the inevitable relationship, or lack there-of, discussion that was about to be set in motion. *Can't you have this talk in the morning?* said the voice in Logan's head, this time not getting its wish.

Chapter 25

"Are you okay?" Jacob asked the next morning, as he noticed Logan acting rather strangely.

"Great," responded Logan enthusiastically as he continued to whistle the tune of the Lion King theme song.

"You're whistling," said Jacob, still very confused about Logan's high spirits.

"And?" responded Logan as he flipped through all the cupboards and drawers in the kitchen.

"You're sure you're alright now, kid?" asked Jacob a second time.

"Never been better, Pops," replied Logan pleasantly as he found the pan he was looking for in the top right corner above the refrigerator and put it onto the stove, then proceeded to crack some egg yolks into the pan.

"Did you already get a response from any of the teams you sent a package out to?" asked Jacob, still trying to figure out what had his son in such good spirits on this morning, which only seemed like a regular day.

"Well, considering that they probably haven't even left the post office yet, I don't think so," Logan responded sarcastically yet pleasantly.

Judging by Logan's almost frightening, but nevertheless lively, demeanour it was pretty safe to assume he had sorted out all "issues" with Samantha the night

The Hockey Farmer

before, and he no longer felt the need to keep quiet about their relationship anymore.

"Dad, I met a girl when I was in Vancouver," said Logan out of the blue. "And I think we're going to try the long distance thing if I end up somewhere other than Vancouver," he added before his father had an opportunity to muster up a response.

"Uhh, is it serious?" Jacob asked the first thing that came to mind.

"Honestly, I don't know," responded Logan truthfully.

"Well, as long as you're happy and it doesn't get in the way of your career, I'm happy, too," said Jacob as he smiled at Logan. "I would like to meet her, though."

"That might be tough, but you will eventually," responded Logan.

"I can wait. Now pass me some of those eggs already," added Jacob passionately as he went to the front door to grab the morning's paper.

Logan and his father worked diligently on the farm from eight o'clock in the morning to anywhere between six o'clock and seven-thirty in the evening for the next seven days straight, including Saturday and Sunday. Logan was back to his normal routine, which consisted of some very hard work that was an incredible means of training for any physical activity, including ice hockey. It was a pretty straightforward life for Logan. Once he came back home after a day on the farm, Logan would jump into the shower right away to eradicate the malodorous smell of manure and cow dung that followed him around all day. After a while, Logan became accustomed to this nauseating scent; however, that didn't mean he enjoyed it, only that he didn't dread it as much as he used to. Following his shower, Logan would sit down for supper with his father and then jump into bed and give Samantha a call. Samantha got off work at five or six o'clock more or less every day, so Logan never had a problem getting a hold of her. Logan would phone her after his evening meal, and they would more often than not talk until the wee hours of the night or even the next morning. And for this reason, Logan convinced his father to integrate a long-distance plan into his cell phone so that the phone bill would be at least somewhat manageable.

However, before Logan even stepped foot into the house after work on any given day, he would check the mail to see if any of the twenty teams he'd sent the package to had replied to his inquiry. After one week, there was still no response from any of the teams. Logan became somewhat anxious, and for that reason, he began to consider the Alberta Junior Hockey League or British Columbia Hockey League. But he'd said he would give the teams from the Canadian Hockey League a two-week window, so he would wait one more week before he sent out the package to these second-tier leagues. It wasn't that Logan was fussy and particular; it was just that he needed a response as soon as possible from any team, or else he would find himself without a place to play for the upcoming season.

On Monday morning, Jacob and Logan were quite optimistic that this would be the day they would finish the restoration of the farm, once and for all. If everything went as planned, all the aspects of the farm would be back on par with the other farms around the area, and that had been Jacob's ultimate goal when he asked Logan to help him at the commencement of the summer. From that point, Jacob could just hire a select group of workers to carry out the required tasks on a daily basis, and then he would be able to lessen his workload drastically and maybe even take a day off every once in a while without worrying about anything. In addition, Logan would be able to leave the farm knowing it was being looked after carefully by a group of professionals, and his father wouldn't be hung out to dry.

Just as Jacob and Logan had originally hoped, everything did go as planned on Monday and as a result, they were ready to make the next step. On Monday evening, when Jacob returned inside from the farm, he gave the agriculture inspectors a call to see if they could come in and give the farm a look. The ultimate goal was to get back their farming license and put the farm back in business. Much to Jacob's surprise and pleasure, the inspectors said they had an open schedule on Tuesday, and they would be able to come in and give the farm a look. For that reason, Jacob went out to the farm again that evening, just to make sure everything was in place and nothing would stop him from receiving the farming license he had longed for these past few years. In the case that the inspectors were not happy with what they saw, they would give Jacob a list of things that needed to be attended to and, strictly following the rules of the agriculture company, they wouldn't be able to come back to the farm for another two months. For that reason, Jacob wanted to make sure everything was spotless and in place.

While Jacob knew Tuesday was going to be a very important day for him personally, little did Logan know that the events of the next day would also turn out to be a

Tuesday to remember for himself, as they would prove to have an everlasting outcome on his happiness—or lack there-of—in the future.

Chapter 26

It wasn't really necessary for Logan to amble around the farm with the inspectors and his father. They would just be walking around the property and taking a look at anything and everything alertly, and if they had any questions, Logan knew his father would be fully capable of answering them proficiently. And after all, Logan was long overdue for a day when he could just loll around in the house and relax without having to worry about anything.

"So, when was this farm originally built?" asked one of several inspectors who had made the trip to analyse and scrutinize every facet of the Watt family farm.

"Well, I inherited it from my father, so it must have been pretty close to seventy-five years ago," recalled Jacob.

Jacob noticed a look of concern on the inspector's face, so he went on.

"But as you can see, we have maintained the farm quite well, and all the systems and machinery have obviously been upgraded on numerous occasions since then," added Jacob, waiting for a reaction from the inspector.

"I see," said the main inspector as he started to walk towards the grading station, which was the most important feature of the farm, closely followed by Jacob and the rest of the inspectors.

As Logan sat on the couch in the living room, he peeked out the window and noticed the group of inspectors, along with his father, were making their way into the grading station.

This is it, Logan thought, as he too knew that if the inspectors thought everything in the grading station was up to par, they would certainly have no problem giving Jacob the farming license he so dearly sought.

Logan continued to peer towards the grading station entrance every once in a while, and after about fifteen long minutes, Logan noticed that everyone was still in the grading station—not one soul had left the building. Logan didn't really know how long these types of inspections usually took, because he had never seen one actually take place.

This can't be good, Logan thought. *Ah, I'm sure everything's alright; they're probably just looking over everything two or three times*, said the voice of reason in Logan's mind.

Or maybe they've found something that was out of place, or maybe I didn't fix the conveyer belt properly, Logan worried. *But I looked over and tested everything like twenty times; everything was perfect*, said the voice of reason in Logan's mind.

Maybe I should go join them, to make sure everything is okay, Logan thought as he continued to peer out the window in the direction of the grading station. *Nah, that would be kind of weird. I'm sure Dad has everything under control*, added the voice of reason as it reassured Logan.

So much for a stress-free day, Logan thought to himself as he turned his attention back to the television rather than the grading station.

"And when and why did you shut down the farm?" asked the main inspector as he pulled out a cloth from his back pocket and proceeded to wipe one of the machines clean, looking for a trace of dirt or dust.

"It was about thirteen years ago," recalled Jacob. "The only reason I shut it down was because I was in no position to run a farm after my wife died, and my son needed me more than the farm did," added Jacob sombrely.

"I'm sorry," responded the inspector.

"Not a problem," said Jacob.

"Sorry for my asking, but couldn't anyone else have run the farm while you took some time off?" asked the main inspector, trying to make sure that Jacob was indeed telling the truth and not making up a story to hide some problem the farm could have had thirteen years ago.

"You're right. Someone could have, and I really considered it," responded Jacob.
"But I knew that even if someone else was running the farm, I would still be stressing over it, and like I said, my son rather than the farm needed my full attention," said Jacob firmly.

"I understand," responded the inspector, once again in a solemn tone. "Sorry for my asking, but I'm just trying to do—" said the inspector as Jacob abruptly interrupted him.

"No, no, don't apologize, you're just doing your job and I completely understand that," said Jacob.

"Thanks," said the main inspector as he waved the rest of the inspectors towards the door.

"What do you think?" asked Jacob excitedly, as it appeared the inspection was complete.

"Well, I think everything looks good, but I'm just the suit. All those guys are the brains behind the business, so I'm going to need to talk it over with them," responded the main inspector as he and Jacob shared a laugh.

"Well, I'll leave you guys to it. I'll just be outside," said Jacob as he opened the door and left the grading station.

Through the living room window, Logan spotted his father leaving the grading station alone. He tried to read his father's body language, but considering that Jacob rarely showed any form of emotion, this was not an easy feat to accomplish, even for Logan. Logan decided to get up off the couch and go talk to his father to determine what was going on.

"Dad," yelled Logan as he opened the living room window and shouted at his father. "What's the deal?" he asked as his father started to walk towards the house.

"Well, they're just talking it over right now, so we should know in a few minutes."

"But what do you think?"

"I don't know, Logan; the main guy said everything looks pretty good, but I don't want to jump to any conclusions and get my hopes up," answered Jacob. "We're just going to have to wait a few minutes. Can you do that, Logan?" added Jacob sternly.

"I know I can, but can you?" asked Logan as he noticed that Jacob was just a little more uneasy than usual.

"Here they come," said Jacob, avoiding the question, as he started to walk back towards the grading station.

Logan closed the window and went back to the couch in the living room, still paying close attention to the conduct of his father and the group of inspectors.

"So are we back in business?" asked Jacob enthusiastically as he walked towards the main inspector.

"Well, there are a few minor issues that definitely need to be attended to before we move forward, but certainly nothing that will get in the way of getting this place running again in the next month or so," responded the main inspector as he held out his hand to Jacob. "Congratulations," he added as he shook Jacob's hand firmly.

"Thanks so much," responded Jacob, glowing with happiness.

"We will fax you the farming license within the next week or so, and then all you'll need to do is sign some papers and fax us back, and from there you can get this show on the road," said the inspector as he put away his papers and started walking towards his car.

"Thanks so much," repeated Jacob for the second time.

"We'll talk to you soon," said the inspector as he got into his car and drove away, followed closely by the four other cars which had been parked on the farm's grounds.

Logan came back to the window as he saw the inspectors drive away. He could tell his father was trying to hide his emotions, but this time, it was fairly obvious that Jacob was very pleased.

"We got it, didn't we?" asked Logan as his father entered the front door of the house.

"We sure did," responded Jacob as he proceeded to give Logan a big tight hug without hesitation. "Thanks to you."

"That's great," said Logan. "But, Dad—"

"Yes, son?" asked Jacob, still firmly embracing Logan.

"I think you can let go of me now," responded Logan.

"Oh, sorry," said Jacob as he finally pulled away.

At the same time that Logan went back to the couch to lie down with the intention of possibly even taking a nap on his day off, the house phone went off.

"I'll get it," yelled Jacob happily as he practically skipped towards the phone in bliss. "It's for you, Logan," he said with an immense smile on his face.

"Ughh," moaned Logan as he got up off the couch. "Who is it?" he asked as he walked towards the kitchen to grab the phone from his father.

"I don't know, someone from Vancouver," responded Jacob pleasantly.

Logan was delighted, because he assumed the Vancouver Giants from the Western Hockey League were calling him to potentially offer him a spot on their team for the upcoming season.

"Hello?" answered Logan.

"Hey, Logan," answered the man, who sounded too much like Coach Vixen from the Vancouver Canucks.

"Coach Vixen?" asked Logan.

"That's me," said the Coach.

"What's up?" asked Logan curiously.

"Well, we talked it over with the management and medical staff, and we've come to the decision that we

The Hockey Farmer

would like to bring you over with us to Victoria for the main training camp with the big boys," answered Coach Vixen in joy.

"You're serious?" said Logan in awe.

"Sure am," responded Coach Vixen. "But this doesn't mean anything permanent; we're giving you another chance because we liked what we saw from you, but with that being said, we didn't see enough of you."

"I understand," replied Logan seriously.

"We'll e-mail you all the information shortly. Get some rest, kid, because I don't want to put any pressure on you, but this could be your last opportunity with the Canucks," said Coach Vixen.

"Yes, sir," answered Logan. "Thanks, Coach."

"Don't thank me; just prove that I was right about you when you get out there on the ice," responded Coach Vixen.

"Yes, sir," repeated Logan.

"Okay, kid," said Coach Vixen as he hung up the phone.

"So?" asked Jacob. He could tell Logan was in shock about the news he had just received.

Logan didn't say a word, not because he didn't want to, but because he hadn't even heard what his father had to say.

"Logan, who was that on the phone?" asked Jacob in a definite and loud voice.

"I'm going to the Vancouver Canucks main training camp," answered Logan, still in awe.

"Does that mean what I think it means?" asked Jacob excitedly.

"Uh, what do you think it means?" asked Logan.

"That you're going to the National Hockey League?"

"Not necessarily."

"Oh," said Jacob. "Well, that's still great new—"

"But I will be going to the National Hockey League," emphasized Logan confidently as he put the phone back on the hook and walked down the hallway into his room.

Chapter 27

"Last call for all passengers for flight 327 to Vancouver, British Columbia," repeated the monotone-voiced P.A announcer in the airport that, after his two previous flights, Logan had become accustomed to.

This time around, Logan wasn't so anxious about the flight itself, considering that last week, he had doubled the total number of airplane trips he had taken throughout his entire life. However, on the other hand, Logan was a lot more nervous about what was going to happen when he arrived at training camp. He'd been the rookie before, with a group of players who were only a few years older than him, and when he arrived in Victoria, he would still be the rookie. However, this time around, he would be going up against some players who had played in the National Hockey League for longer than the duration of his life. The only thing that that kept Logan somewhat calm and composed was the fact that he'd be there with Frank Dempster, who would also be going to his first National Hockey League training camp. Also, Logan had already met Todd Lang—who was one of the main leaders of the Canucks—at the team dinner during the prospects week, and Todd had been very respectful and friendly.

Hopefully they're all like that, Logan thought as he took his first-class seat on the airplane.

Logan had sat in the business-class section on his last two flights courtesy of the Vancouver Canucks organization, and he'd been treated with nothing but respect and esteem by the organization once he arrived in Vancouver for the duration of the week. However, this time Logan was pleased to find that he was sitting in the first class section.

I hope this is a sign of things to come, Logan thought as he strapped on his seatbelt and the plane took flight soon after.

Logan didn't fall asleep on the way to Vancouver, since he wasn't about to deal with that embarrassment for a second time. He simply watched Sportsnet Connected on the mini-television attached to the seat directly in front of him. Once he arrived in Vancouver, despite what Logan would have liked, there would be a driver waiting to drive him directly to the Horseshoe Bay terminal, where he would meet all of the other players and then take the ferry to Victoria. Logan would have liked to see Samantha before he left, but the Canucks were pretty strict about their time tables, and he didn't want to miss the ferry just so he could see Samantha for a few minutes and satisfy his needs.

As Logan hopped into the limo waiting for him at the Vancouver airport, he remembered that Frank Dempster was already on the island since he lived in Nanaimo, so he would in all probability just meet the team in Victoria rather than take the ferry with them. Frank had told him Nanaimo was about a two-hour drive from Victoria, so it would make no sense for him to take the ferry to Vancouver and then go back to Victoria when he could just go directly there from his hometown.

That means Todd is the only guy I know who's going to be on the ferry, Logan thought as the driver pulled out of the airport parking lot and merged onto the freeway. *Well, aside from Luke, of course*, Logan recalled. He hoped Luke would tone down his hostility now that he'd be around some true professionals like Todd Lang.

When Logan arrived at the ferry terminal about an hour later, he saw a group of men standing out front autographing anything from jerseys to hockey cards. It was pretty clear that these were the Vancouver Canucks. These were the men he would be going up against to earn his spot on the team. Logan's suspicions were confirmed when he saw Coach Vixen talking to Todd Lang and Sean Townsend, the three men standing next to the big group of fans getting their memorabilia autographed by the players.

"Ah damn, someone must have tipped off the fans or media," said the limo driver as he looked at all of the people covered in Canucks merchandise. "You better get used to this type of stuff, especially when you get down to Victoria," he said as he handed Logan his suitcase.

"Thanks for the heads up," said Logan as he started to walk towards Coach Vixen, Todd, and Sean. "Oh, and thanks for the ride," added Logan as he turned back and waved at the driver.

Logan was somewhat relieved that most of the guys slept on the ferry ride to Victoria, because he wasn't really in the mood to socialize. When he met the group before they boarded the ferry, they all seemed pretty cool, yet none of them really stood out as being overly friendly or social. However, some of the guys, including Todd Lang, decided to head out to the sun deck about halfway through the ride, so Logan decided to join them.

Wow, this is beautiful, Logan thought as he looked at the ocean and mountains from atop the sun deck of the ferry.

"Isn't it beautiful, Logan?" asked Todd as he pulled his digital camera from his backpack.

"It's amazing," answered Logan as he stepped out of the way so Todd could take his picture. "You're definitely going to have to e-mail me these pictures—I didn't even think about bringing a camera," he added, still amazed by the beautiful view of the scenery.

"For sure," answered Todd as he continued to snap some pictures from several different angles. "So Logan, Coach Vixen just told me you're going to be rooming with me once we get to Victoria," he added as he pressed the menu button on his camera to see the pictures he had just taken.

"Oh, really?" asked Logan, surprised yet overjoyed.

"Yup—well, he actually gave me a choice out of the rookies, and I chose you," responded Todd.

"Oh yeah, and why is that?" asked Logan as he laughed quietly.

"Honestly, I really don't know," replied Todd as he started to snap some more pictures again. "I guess it's because you're an Alberta boy just like me," he added as he started to walk down to deck to get some different angles.

Logan laughed again.

"Well, I'm glad to hear it, since you're pretty much the only guy I know here—aside from Frank and Luke, obviously," said Logan truthfully.

Todd laughed. "Oh, don't worry, you'll get to know all of the guys sooner or later, and even though it might not have seemed like it today, most of them are nicer than I am."

I doubt that, Logan thought but refrained from saying it. "Yeah, they all seem pretty cool, but that will probably all change once we get on the ice, won't it?" he asked.

"Well, they all get pretty intense, but I guess that's to be expected," answered Todd. "But with that said, all of them will keep it clean, so I wouldn't worry about getting injured again," he added.

"That's comforting," said Logan.

"Yeah, but I heard Luke Brown had it out for you at prospects camp there, eh?" said Todd.

"I guess you could say that," said Logan as he looked at his fully healed left wrist.

Todd shook his head in disgust.

"Don't worry about that guy here either; he won't try any of that stuff with the big boys around him. The guys here keep it clean, but if someone like him starts running around and going after anyone, they will take exception," said Todd as Logan once again felt reassured.

"Good to hear," responded Logan.

"And Logan, if you have any questions at all once we get down to Victoria, no matter how stupid they may seem, don't hesitate to ask me," said Todd.

"Thanks, man—yeah, I'm sure I'll have more than a few."

"I would certainly hope so. Well, we should probably get downstairs. I think we're going to dock any minute now," added Todd as he looked towards the harbour and then started to pack up his camera.

Logan, Todd and the rest of the group decided to leave the ferry from the vehicle level rather than the passenger level because they had been given word that hundreds of fans were awaiting them at the other side of the passenger exit. Most of the guys were exhausted and just wanted to get settled in the hotel, and since they'd already spent a fair bit of time autographing before they boarded the ferry, they decided they would try to avoid another session. Their plan worked to perfection. The team arrived at the Bear Mountain Inn without being recognized by a single soul. Coach Vixen informed the group that there would be a team meeting later in the evening, after everyone got to meet their roommates and got settled in to their rooms.

Todd's calm, cool and collected persona started to rub off on Logan throughout the day. Logan felt much more relaxed being around someone who didn't feel any anxiety and seemed to have an answer for every question. In general, the whole feeling around the players here at the main training camp was much different from that of the players at the prospects tryout. Here in Victoria, even though most of the players, including Todd, were excited to start a new season, they just acted as if this training camp was simply another day on the job. At prospects camp, most of the players, including Logan, were overwhelmed by the treatment they were receiving.

"Logan, which bed do you want?" asked Todd as he and Logan walked into their room, which looked fairly similar to Logan's room at the Fairmont Hotel in Vancouver.

The Hockey Farmer

"Oh, it doesn't matter to me," answered Logan respectfully, even though he preferred the bed next to the balcony.

"Me neither, and I'm not good with making decisions, so just pick one already," said Todd.

Logan chuckled. "Alright, I'll take this one," he said as he threw his bag on the bed next to the balcony.

"Good, I was hoping you would choose that one," said Todd as he put his suitcase down and hopped onto his bed.

Logan chuckled again and promptly followed suit by lying down on his bed. He peered over at Todd and noticed he had already dozed off.

Maybe I should take a nap, too; there's nothing else to do anyways, Logan thought as he closed his eyes.

As he lay motionless on his bed with his eyes shut, Logan visualized what he wanted out of the upcoming week in Victoria. He pictured himself scoring goals, and scoring a lot of them. He imagined duplicating his end-to-end rush from the scrimmage at the prospects tryout last week. He pictured himself out-working every other player on the ice every single shift and not holding anything back. And lastly, Logan visualized himself making the team and ultimately donning the Vancouver Canucks jersey.

Chapter 28

"For those of you who are new here," Coach Vixen began at the early morning team meeting. Most of the group peered over towards Logan and Frank. "This isn't like most training camps you've probably attended, due to the time constraints of the National Hockey League Schedule. We have two on-ice sessions to see what you're made of, and after that we have to decide which of you to bring along to our exhibition games."

Even though this was Logan's first professional training camp, he was aware that they didn't usually last more then two or three days. If you made the cut in this short time, then you would have to prove yourself at the next step—which, as Coach Vixen explained, was the exhibition games against real opponents. If you were still hanging around by the time the exhibition games had come to an end, then you would know you were in pretty good shape.

"If anyone comes to you directly asking for an interview, be sure to tell them to go through our media guy, P.K. Campbell. Well, time is really of the essence, so let's get this show on the road," said Coach Vixen as the entire group migrated from the conference room—which was designed more as a lounge—at the Bear Mountain Arena to the two dressing rooms.

Logan was surprised to see most of the veterans were proceeding in a loose and almost lackadaisical manner as they prepared to hit the ice. He'd expected an intense atmosphere similar to that at the prospects camp, but it was almost the complete opposite. Most of the guys were making jokes about the most unusual things; they were all just going through the motions and sincerely having a good time.

"This reminds me of my elementary school recess," said Frank as Logan chuckled and continued to put his equipment on. "I'll see you out there," added Frank, and he picked up both of his sticks off the rack and started towards the ice surface.

Logan noticed that some of the others started to do the same. The laid-back attitude in the room got the best of Logan; he found himself focusing on what the others were talking about instead of what should have been on his mind: Hockey. Logan quickly finished tying his skates and proceeded to put his upper body equipment on. He strapped on his helmet and took a moment to get in the right mindset before he stepped foot on the ice. Logan picked up his sticks and walked down the tunnel towards the ice, but not before he recited his customary prayer under his breath.

"Since we only have two days to see what you're all made of, we're not going to waste time skating you," said Coach Vixen at center ice as a wave of excitement overtook the players. "But you all sure as hell better be in shape, and this only means that you're going to need to go even harder in all the drills," added the Coach as the wave excitement significantly died down.

Even though Logan and Frank were the rookies of the group, they both felt as though they had somewhat of an advantage since they had been consistently skating for a few weeks, while for many of the veterans this would be the first time they skated hard all summer.

"Alright, so we're just going to do a couple of drills here, then we'll jump right into scrimmage. After all, we really only care about how you perform in game situations," said Coach Vixen as Logan and Frank listened attentively to each word that came out of his mouth.

This was music to Logan's ears. He absolutely detested most drills; he felt that they didn't do him any justice. He knew he really shined when he was playing in an actual game.

Logan was surprised when Coach Vixen informed the group they were to do a full ice Philly drill followed by the three-on-three down low drill, just as they had during the prospects camp. He'd expected to have to do some more complicated drills which he'd never done before, but he turned out to be wrong.

"This isn't so bad after all," said Frank as he skated passed Logan.

Logan felt the same way. However, they both soon realized that even though they were doing the same drills, it was a far cry from what they had been doing with the other prospects. The speed and tempo were overwhelming, all the passes were crisp and to the tape, the three-man cycle was executed to a tee, and last but certainly not least, the intensity level was far greater than Logan and Frank had thought was even possible with such a simple drill. When the three-on-three drill finally came to an end, Logan was already exhausted. He was looking for anything to motivate and rejuvenate him for the upcoming scrimmage, and as his eyes wandered off into the crowd, Logan found what he was looking for. It was Samantha. She had her voice recorder out and was looking over her notes, so she appeared to be there on official business; however, Logan was still thrilled to see she'd made the trip. Samantha looked up and waved at Logan excitedly, but he simply nodded back—he didn't want to risk looking like an immature adolescent by waving back like someone in *Pee Wee* would do.

"Nolan, Morris, and, uhh, Watt, you're up next," said Coach Vixen as he paced back and forth on the players' bench.

"Who's playing down the middle, Coach?" asked Brad Morris, Vancouver's second line left winger.

"Uhh, Watt, can you play center this shift?" asked Coach Vixen as he realized he had made a slight blunder by putting three wingers on the same line.

"Sure, Coach," said Logan immediately.

Logan did have some experience playing at the center position, but not a lot. Back in Cochrane, Logan used to play center on the penalty kill, but that was about it. On the penalty kill, both forwards were supposed to stay somewhere in the vicinity of the opposing defenders, atop the four-man box, so it really didn't make a difference as to who was playing center or on the wing. But it was entirely different at even strength, since that was when the center really had to come back down low into his own end to help out the defence-men along the boards. Despite Logan's lack of experience playing center, he wasn't about to turn down the Coach and tell him he was incapable of playing the position. As the puck was dumped deep into the opposing team's zone, all three forwards on Logan's team changed on the fly, so he, Mark Nolan, and Brad Morris simultaneously jumped over the boards and skated into the play. Logan turned on the jets and initiated the fore-check by angling out the opposing defender and forcing him to move the puck along the boards, where Brad Morris was waiting. Morris intercepted the pass and made a quick head fake before he fired the puck on net. As Logan skated towards the net, looking for a rebound, he saw the loose puck sitting right in front of the goaltender, so he promptly pounced on it and put it in the back of the net. Logan scored the first goal of the scrimmage, but not before he was cross-checked by Matt Orr, Vancouver's bruising defence-man. Logan's back was sore for the rest of the scrimmage, but the pain suddenly went away when the final buzzer went off and Logan realized that he had scored the only goal of the game.

"Logan, how does it feel to be the hero on day one of training camp here in Victoria?" said a familiar voice as Logan entered the dressing room after the practice had concluded.

"Well, Samantha, I wouldn't classify myself as the hero at all, because you know both teams played hard and there wasn't an inch to be had out there. I was fortunate enough to capitalize on a rebound there in the first, but, uh, I guess I was just in the right place at the right time," Logan replied.

"Thanks for giving me a typical hockey player answer," said Samantha as she put away her recorder.

"Any time," said Logan with a big smile on his face.

"You played great," said Samantha as she embraced Logan.

"Thanks; hopefully the Coaches thought so too," responded Logan as he and Samantha separated.
"Don't worry; I'm sure they did. But Logan…"
"Yeah?"
"You really need to take a shower."

Chapter 29

"Logan, can I speak to you for a minute?" Coach Vixen asked the next morning, as the players prepared for their second and final on-ice session at General Motors Place.

"Sure, Coach," Logan stopped taping his stick and followed Coach Vixen out of the dressing room.

"Alright, well, here's the deal, kid: We love what we have seen from you, and we think you have the tools to play at the next level."

Please don't say but, Logan thought.

"But the thing is, we already have our same four wingers from last year secured on our top two lines, and we wouldn't want you playing on the 3rd or 4th line," said Coach Vixen as Logan remained silent. "It wouldn't benefit us, and it certainly wouldn't benefit you. If anything, playing less than 10 minutes a night with a bunch of grinders would only stunt your development rather than improve it," Coach Vixen went on.

Logan was speechless.

"However, we would still like to keep you in the system and if you're interested, you could play with our minor league team down in Manitoba," added Coach Vixen.

The Hockey Farmer

Logan wasn't about to turn down an opportunity to play professional hockey, even if it wasn't at the elite level.

"Yeah, for sure, I'd love to," answered Logan, still evidently disappointed.

"Perfect, and I can assure you that you'll be one of the first we look at if we get into injury trouble up here in Vancouver," said Coach Vixen.

"Sounds good; so should I still hit the ice with the guys, or no?"

"Go home and get some rest, Logan. We'll let you know about the arrangements for Manitoba later today," answered Coach Vixen.

"Alright," said Logan as he walked back towards the dressing room to pick up his equipment.

"Hey Logan!" yelled Coach Vixen before Logan reached the dressing room.

"Yeah?"

"Would you call Dempster out here?"

"Sure, Coach," answered Logan as he entered the dressing room, wondering if Frank was about to receive the same news that he just did.

Logan went back into the room, grabbed his two sticks off the rack, picked up his hockey bag, and told Frank that Coach Vixen was waiting for him in the hall. A few eyebrows were raised by some of the veterans in the room as they soon realized that Logan had been cut from the Vancouver Canucks. The irrelevant banter in the room rapidly died down as Logan made his way to the exit.

"Logan, each and every one of us in this room has been cut at one point or another. But don't worry; your time will come," said Todd, and the others agreed.

"Thanks, Todd," answered Logan as be began to say his goodbyes to the rest of the group.

"So I'm assuming you're going down to Manitoba?" asked Brad Morris from across the room.

"Yeah," answered Logan.

"Well, I'm sure we'll see you back up here at some point this season," added Mark Nolan, who was in the process of tying his skates.

"I sure hope so," responded Logan as he once again started towards the exit.

Before Logan left the room, he heard a voice calling his name that he didn't even recognize.

"Hey, Logan," said the voice as Logan turned around and saw the bruising defenceman Matt Orr.

"Yeah?" answered Logan, wishing this awkward moment would end at once.

"Sorry about that cross-check yesterday," said Matt sincerely.

"No problem, man, I'll see ya guys later," answered Logan as he was finally able to leave the room.

You could say anything you wanted about these professional National Hockey League players on the ice, but Logan soon realized that no one could ever question their class and dignity off it.

I can't imagine Luke Brown ever apologizing for a dirty play, Logan thought as he chuckled and exited the Bear Mountain arena.

Frank Dempster arrived at the hotel only minutes after Logan, which confirmed Logan's suspicions that Frank was also released from the team. However, Logan soon discovered that Frank would not be joining him in Manitoba. Coach Vixen had informed Frank that they would like him to play a season in the Western Hockey League before they brought him into the system. Frank was very disappointed, but just like Logan, he remained optimistic that he would one day play in the National Hockey League. Later that afternoon, Logan received his itinerary for his flight to Manitoba. He would be leaving first thing the next morning to embark on yet another journey in his eventful rollercoaster-like summer. Much to Logan's displeasure, Samantha was working late that night, so he didn't even have the opportunity to bid his farewell.

Once Logan arrived in Winnipeg, Manitoba the next morning, he was ushered directly to the MTS Center, where he would be taking part in his third training camp of the summer: The main Manitoba Moose training camp in Winnipeg. The Manitoba Moose were the Vancouver Canucks' American Hockey League affiliate team. The Moose were essentially part of the Canucks organization, since the Canucks had access to all of their players if need be. Even though Coach Vixen had informed Logan that they would like him to play with the Moose in Manitoba this season, he still needed to perform well at camp to secure his spot on the team. This time around, Logan went into camp with a stress-free approach, which he'd picked up from Todd and the rest of the players in Vancouver. Early on at camp, it seemed to be working for him.

Just as he had in his previous two training camps, Logan impressed all the coaches in Manitoba with, first and foremost, his speed. Logan held his own in all the drills and was arguably the top forward in the traditional intra-squad game, scoring a goal and recording two assists, even though his team lost 6-5. Once training camp had concluded and Logan was still with the group, he become conscious of the fact that in all likelihood, he would start the season with the Manitoba Moose. Before Manitoba's first exhibition game, Luke Brown joined the group as he too was released by the Vancouver Canucks.

Just my luck, Logan as he picked up his stick off the rack and began to tape it in preparation for his first real game of the season.

But it appeared to be a case of déjà vu all over again as Manitoba's Head Coach, Steven Adams, entered the room.

"Logan, can you come outside for a second?" asked Coach Adams. Logan wondered if maybe his thoughts of satisfaction were premature.

"Sure, Coach," answered Logan as he followed Coach Adams out of the room.

"I actually don't know what this is about, but Don Gale is on the line, and he wants to speak to you. The phone's just in my office," said Coach Adams as he pointed to the door across the hall.

"Don Gale as in *the* Don Gale, the General Manager of the Canucks?" Logan asked in disbelief.

"That's the one, and I probably wouldn't want to keep him waiting," answered Coach Adams.

"Right," said Logan as he entered the Coach's office without hesitation.

This could be the call, Logan thought as he took a deep breath and picked up the phone.

"Hi, Don," said Logan.

"Hey, Logan. Now, I don't know if you heard what happened or not, but Brad Morris was severely injured earlier this morning," said Don.

The Hockey Farmer

"Really? No, I haven't heard anything; what happened?" asked Logan.

"Well, he was going hard into the corner in the intra-squad game this morning, and he lost an edge and fell heavily into the boards," responded the General Manager of the Vancouver Canucks.

That's horrible, Logan thought. "How's he doing?" he asked.

"Not good—early reports are that he may have a broken leg. He'll be out for at the very least two months."

"That's unfortunate," said Logan, as he started to wonder if Don was just giving him a debriefing session, or if he had anything significant to say.

"It's unfortunate for everyone except you, because we want you to take his place for the time being," said Don in a subtle manner.

Logan was thrilled, but he didn't want to seem overly excited, because this opportunity came at the expense of the well-being of Brad Morris.

"I won't let you down," said Logan finally in a voice that reeked of sheer professionalism.

"That's good to hear. Your flight is already booked for later tonight, so when you get here, we'll work out all your contract details," said Don.

"Looking forward to it," answered Logan genuinely.

"Alright, kid," said Don as he hung up the phone.

Logan took a moment to digest the delightful information he had just received and then made his way back into the dressing room to pack up his equipment yet again.

"Where you off to now?" asked one of the players in the dressing room as Logan started to pick up his hockey bag.

"Brad Morris got injured in Vancouver's intra-squad game this morning. I'm going to the NHL," replied Logan, still trying to let the news sink in.

"Congratulations, bud," said Mattias Karlsson, Manitoba's captain, in his soothing Swedish accent.

"Thanks," said Logan, and the others began to congratulate him as well.

"Good luck this season, boys," said Logan as he picked up his sticks off the rack and began to walk towards the exit.

"Hey, Watter," said Luke Brown, an unexpected yet familiar voice.

"Yeah," answered Logan, just waiting for one of Luke's spiteful and tactless comments.

"Congratulations," he said.

Logan waited a moment to see if Luke was going to drop in some sort of sarcastic line afterwards, but it didn't happen.

"Thanks," answered Logan, realizing that this was the first genuine conversation he'd ever had with Luke.

"Yeah, so I guess this is the end of the road for you then, eh," added Luke.

Logan took another moment before he answered. "I guess so," he said. "Take it easy, boys," added Logan as he left the room.

As Logan hopped on the flight to beautiful Vancouver, British Columbia later that night, he thought about Luke's last words. Logan knew that in a sense, this was the end of the road for him. His lifelong goal had been to play in the National Hockey League, and he was on the verge of accomplishing that goal. But in another sense, Logan knew he had yet to accomplish anything of significance at the elite level. So this wasn't the end of the road for him—it was just the beginning.

About the Author

Ever heard the saying "Behind every sports writer is a frustrated athlete?" Well that sentiment unquestionably rings true with this proud native of Nanaimo, British Columbia. Farhan Devji played organized ice hockey with both the Nanaimo Minor Hockey Association and the Port Moody Amateur Hockey Association until grade twelve, and also played basketball up until the tenth grade, before he realized that he would be better suited to write about sports rather than to play them.

Farhan's two biggest passions are sports and writing, which works out perfectly as he likes to combine the two together. He is an avid Vancouver Canucks supporter and has an incurable infatuation with the game of hockey. Farhan enjoys writing Young Adult novels which focus primarily, but not exclusively, on sports. He would one day like to become a recognized and respected author and/or journalist in his community.

The Hockey Farmer is Farhan's first published novel, however, "it's the first of many." Farhan loves to hear from his readers, so check out his website—
(www.farhandevji.com)
Or send him an email at fdevji@gmail.com.

Cacoethes Publishing House, LLC.
(cacoethes=uncontrollable desire)

Action/Adventure
Fantasy
Historical
Horror
Mainstream
Mystery/Suspense
Non-Fiction
Paranormal
Romance
Science Fiction
Western
And Much, Much More!

http://www.cacoëthespublishing.com

Farhan Devji

The Hockey Farmer

Printed in the United States
119852LV00001B/63/P